Tyne O'Connell, screenwriter and novelist, hails from an artworld background. She is married to the conceptual artist Eric Hewitson, and divides her time between LA and London. Tyne O'Connell is the author of *Sex, Lies and Litigation*, *Latest Accessory*, *What's A Girl To Do?* and *Making the A-List*.

That Girl–Boy Thing

Tyne O'Connell

review

First published in 2001
by REVIEW

An imprint of Headline Book Publishing

10 9 8 7 6 5 4 3 2 1

ISBN 0 7472 7170 4

Typeset by Palimpsest Book Production Limited,
Polmont, Stirlingshire
Printed and bound in Great Britain by
Clays Ltd, St Ives plc.

Headline Book Publishing
A division of Hodder Headline
338 Euston Road
London NW1 3BH

www.reviewbooks.co.uk
www.hodderheadline.com

Acknowledgements

It was Nancy Lublin who inspired me to set a book in New York and dragged me around the Village and Tribeca, hooking me up with the right places and right people. I am now two tattoos and bags of attitude better off. Thanks also to the girls who kept me sane during the writing process: Faith Salie, Tricia Davie, Ava Fabian, Wendy Goldman, Alicia Gordon, Nicole Clemens, and the ever glamorous Cordelia. Without giving their cover away, I also have to thank the guys who helped me with the Boy Stuff and who were decent and indiscreet enough to reveal the arcane knowledge of what it is that makes guys tick. To S.P. Nick Holly, Justin Pike, Albert Sutherland, Matt, and doormen, taxi drivers and barmen everywhere. Guys – you really are a very sick bunch. Thanks a million.

CHAPTER ONE

My mother tells me that lingerie is my substitute for dating. I meet a nice pair of knickers on the sale table. I tell myself I'll die if I don't make them mine. I even fight another girl for them (well, they're worth it); besides, they'll make my life complete in a way nothing else can. Even if they are a little on the small side. With my self-determined style, I'll be able to transform them. Posing in my knickers in the mirror for the first time, I decide we look great together. In the beginning it is true love – party after party I wash them tenderly by hand. After a while, though, we start staying in, eating popcorn by the television and clipping our nails. Soon I get bored and restless and start loitering with intent around the lingerie stores again. Eventually, despite the fun we've had together, I ruthlessly come to the decision that they just don't fit into my life anymore. They are too demanding.

Extract from the 'New York Girl' column of Anna Denier

Anna

Restaurant loos are the new cultural hot-spots, the new French cafés, the new chat rooms, the new members' clubs of our time. Think about it; behind the lipstick and the spritzing, very important matters are discussed in restrooms – lives are changed even!

Decisions on whether to sleep with a guy, flirt with a guy or dump a guy are made. For instance, last night in the loo at the Tribeca Grill, someone asked me a question that really got me thinking about my future. 'Do you know,' they inquired, looking at me earnestly like they truly cared, 'where you're *really* going?'

Existential or what?

'Hey, that's not the sort of weighty issue you want to dive into when you're dying for a waz,' I told him, throwing the full force of my fatal charm at him.

Thing is, I've never really planned my future, see. When I was a teenager I couldn't predict what I'd be doing that night, let alone the rest of my life. And you know what, I like it that way. Once I know where

I'm going it will mean that I'm, well, one of those grown-up people.

Actually, I think the guy was just wondering what a girl was doing in the men's restroom, but still, it got me thinking. In fact, after a bit of light to medium flirting over by the basins, I dragged him home to help me with my ponderings.

Now, before you get the idea that I'm the sort of girl who hangs out in places like the Tribeca Grill and drags home guys I meet in restrooms all the time, the sort of girl with loads of money and sass, I'm going to have to disabuse you. I'm a weekly columnist, which is *so* last year I know, but, incredible as it seems, my opinions are highly valued and eagerly sought by millions. Which is kind of sad given that I live and work alone in a one-bedroom apartment on Hudson, wearing a tired old Wonderbra that has long since lost its wonder, an unlit Camel cigarette permanently glued to my lower lip (lighting them causes cancer, see), and a pair of faux-fur cat's ears I like to kid myself make me look cute.

A girl can dream.

These days people tell me I should give up wearing cigarettes, but I'm only twenty years old for heaven's sake. okay, so twenty-something if we are going to split the atom. But still, that's way too immature to start giving things up, especially if I'm going to live to be one hundred and thirty.

Sometimes I feel like an adolescent trapped in a body ageing without my consent – it's as if life is passing me by and giving me the finger. Bald creepy men no longer forgive me quite so quickly when I accidentally spill my drink on them. Taxi drivers don't ignore other people hailing them in order to stop for me. Barmen certainly don't give me free drinks anymore, and I've read the books and been to the chat rooms and it's only going to get worse.

Other people notice the changes before you, apparently. You just start analysing stuff you once simply took for granted. Noticing things that you never noticed before, i.e. the self-help shelves at Borders. I never knew that you could *Tap Into The Real You*. I'm still not certain that there *is* a real me, and even if there is, I'm not sure we'd get on.

Suddenly, though, these self-help titles seem to be speaking directly to me, which is scary because you only have to look at the ends of my overly coloured hair to see that I am the *last* person who should be allowed to self-help. They should post staff at the self-help section to steer girls like me away. 'Move along there, luv,' the security guys should say. 'Why don't you go take a browse round the children's books where you can't hurt yourself?'

Since the guy last night in the toilet got me thinking, I've been trying to conjure up a long-term plan for my future; you know, something beyond waiting for a new ice-cream flavour to be invented or a hair bleach that doesn't sting. I really should be channelling more enthusiasm into my career, I suppose. Get a plan. Get one of those life thingamees like that junkie in *Trainspotting* did. It's just that I'm really busy and I don't know where I'd fit a life into my schedule, along with all the other stuff like cocktails, shopping, openings and wishful thinking.

And anyway, my interest usually flags before I've finished my morning quad-shot latte. I just can't see the point. Striving really takes it out of me, and do I even want a place in the East Hamptons overlooking Calvin Klein's? I've got the underwear, isn't that enough?

I'm *so* over upward mobility. I mean, what's so great about being mobile? I really like staying still; wasting time lying in bed watching *I Love Lucy* for a day is my idea of heaven. And anyway, the traffic on the way to the E. Hamptons is *merde*.

Sienna, the girl who lives downstairs (real blonde, real breasts and v. pos. attitude), is on a quest for answers and fulfilment. That's how she staves off disillusionment, she tells me.

But I'm not looking for a guru. I'm mainlining

disillusionment quite happily. It's one of the last vices still legal out there. And as for answers, I'm still struggling to find a decent question. Answers, along with cellulite, the United Nations and 'isms' generally, are v. last millennium, I tell Sienna. I also make a mental note to point this out to my readers in my next column. Questions are the new hope, I'll tell them. Coming up with new questions, like why is it easier to get a gun than a Valium in this town? People need calming down more than they need a license to kill, surely?

Somedays, as I reposition a loose pad in my Wonderbra and munch into a bowl of Captain Crunch, I almost feel unworthy of the title Twenty-Something, conjuring as it does images of girls in charge of their destinies, girls who can talk their careers up at dinner parties, girls with throaty laughs, real-cleavage and functional relationships. Girls who eat salad – and mean it. Girls who would be able to answer the question 'Where are you going?' without pausing for breath.

Sienna and I talk about this stuff quite a bit because, despite our differences, we're good for one another. For starters, no one else could tell me that I'm afraid of growing up and not get squirted with my Astro Girl water pistol.

I think she's judging me by my apartment. A child-sized one-bedroom on Hudson with *Sesame Street* foam flooring in the bathroom, floor-to-ceiling shoes in the bedroom, and loads of hip eighties designer ashtrays (and you thought there weren't any). There are various accessories giving testimony to my madly delusional nature: a pair of black-feather angel's wings here, an eight-inch-high pair of joggers there, and a box of Lego in a corner. Framed pictures of Ernie, Miss Piggy and Alice in Wonderland represent my mentors. It's not that I loved my childhood so much that I didn't want to let it go. Quite the opposite really, it's my childhood that dug its claws into me!

Another thing that my life is littered with is exes. Ex-bosses, ex-parents, ex-agents, ex-boyfriends, ex-fads. I'm always escaping from the grasp of love, jobs, bills and savings plans. I sense an adult aspiration coming on and I move town – well, that's my mother's story. Sienna shakes her head at this. She wants kids, commitment and immortality (in that order). There is so much we don't share.

Apart from the fear that my Madeleine doll might abandon me for my own offspring, I don't actually think kids these days are looking for a girl like me to nurture them through their formative years. I'm way too immature for motherhood.

I still sniff those perfume peel-backs in magazines.

I still read *Vogue* while sitting on the toilet.

I still dream of driving down Fifth Avenue in the Pope–mobile. (It just looks so cool and safe.)

I still believe that a new bra really could change my life.

I still have casual sex. (Last night, for instance.)

I still haven't arrived at the January sales on time yet.

And what kid wants to depend on a girl like me on parent and teacher nights?

My friends back in London on the other hand have started grabbing unsuitable partners and charging down the aisle like lemmings. Some of them are already pregnant which is *so* depressing.

It was this increasing ratio of married-with-hope-of-kids-in-the-future friendships that provoked my move away from London, where I'd been living since I was sixteen. If the girls that made Notting Hill all it was were giving up casual sex and martinis, I was out of there. New city, new job, new apartment, new friends, new bills, new lovers. I'm a bit like one of those guys who sell their car because the ashtray's full.

But enough of me. Fact is, I've scored. Yeah, me, the original short-straw-puller in romance, dragged home the sort of guy every girl alive fantasises about. Seriously, if he was ever strapped for cash – which he isn't by the way – he could score a part on *All My*

Children. Don't laugh, it's true. I am looking at the proof right now – an indent beside me on the bed. I can hear the shower going so he's still here, in my Girl Zone. I reach out and put my hand on the sheet to absorb the molecules of his presence. Comforted, I fall back into a deep sleep.

CHAPTER TWO

Contraception sexed women up. It gave us options beyond our previously assigned role as mothers. It started with the pill, followed by the morning-after pill, and finally legalised abortion. By then we were hooked; we discovered the clitoral orgasm, the vaginal orgasm, the G-spot. It was blissful. After centuries of saying 'No' we started saying 'Yes! Yes! Don't stop!'.

It was a relief to be confronted with Dolly the sheep, the first cloned animal. And to top it off, Arnold Schwarzenegger fell pregnant in Junior *and actually declared, 'My Body My Choice'. Finally, after years of protest, men are showing a willingness to share the ordeal of gestation and childbirth.*

If babies can be grown in test-tubes and the bodies of Hollywood's leading men, where does this leave women? Free to pursue more pleasurable activities like cocktails, that's where.

Extract from *I'll Have Mine On The Rocks!* by Topsy Denier

Mark

I am sitting on the toilet in the apartment of the coolest girl I've ever met, wondering how I can cleave myself to her life for a little longer. It's pathetic I know. I only met her last night and even though she hasn't asked me to leave yet, I sensed by the way she was kicking me in her sleep that she plans to.

Normally this would be fine by me. I love disposable sex as much as the next guy, but this girl is different. I don't want the inevitable 'look-it-was-great-last-night-but . . .' speech with this girl. I know that I haven't known her that long, but you don't need to know someone long to be intrigued do you? And when that intrigue comes with a hard-on, it can make you want crazy things. Well, that's my story and I'm sticking to it.

Maybe it's because this girl is a variation on my usual type? Not just because of the way she looks (hot) or dresses (wild) or talks with a really cool British accent (cool); there is something chemical about the effect she has on me – something combustible.

See, the way I figure it, it all comes down to commitment prospects. As in, they want it, I don't. All the girls I've ever met have been obsessed with where a relationship is going. You can tell when a girl is sniffing out your long-term prospects. And yeah, I know that remark is about as sexist a statement as a guy can make with his gonads intact, but I can't help it. I have to stand by this theory. Girls are into prospects the way guys are into breasts. Girls don't want to waste time mucking around in a relationship without a future. They're practical like that. I can see the sense in their attitude, but not many guys in their twenties are into their own futures, let alone the future of a girl their groin is screaming out to sleep with. Once the sex is over, once a guy has conquered and the knot is in the condom, his commitment to a girl begins to wane.

Even now, at twenty-nine, I'm not really in the market for someone to spend my dotage with. Take Rebecca, one of my best friends in college. She never took me seriously because I couldn't give her a clear indication of where the relationship was going. She wanted a map, a plan, a sure thing. And I was already looking to get lost inside another girl's body.

If I ever get married, however – and I guess

statistically it is inevitable that I will – I want to marry someone just like Rebecca, which is weird. Not that we ever said The Words or had That Conversation, but she was great to hang out with. The best time was when we were on a kibbutz together during a summer break at college. But it was never, I repeat, never, a Serious Thing. Bec's a girl I can have fun with. She gets who I am, see – a pretty okay guy, with low to medium level asshole tendencies.

Yet Rebecca and I were like those really boring lab experiments at school where nothing blows up. We had just about everything that makes a supposedly perfect relationship, minus the vital ingredient – passion. We had the same taste in music (which seemed to mean a lot more in college), the same political views; we even rooted for the same ball team. The only other problem was the laugh factor. Even though we shared a similar sense of humour, she never actually made me laugh. Only I hadn't realised that. Until now.

See that's the thing; meeting Anna has already made me discover stuff about my life and myself that I never knew before. Portentous, that's how it feels.

'Fuck!'

I am looking at a picture of Ernie on the wall. You know Ernie, as in Bert and Ernie? I feel my face redden. This means Ernie saw me take a crap earlier, this means Ernie witnessed my shower. Ernie saw me naked. I can hear him cackling away in that wheezy laugh of his. I suddenly feel very weird because although it hasn't occurred to me in years, Ernie was one of my idols as a kid and I never ever wanted him to see that side of me. I hope he doesn't rat about it to Bert. That would be too much.

Getting back to Anna. I met her last night at the Tribeca Grill. It was Rob and Rebecca's engagement party. I dunno; Rob is one of my oldest friends and all that, but even though he's a great guy, I'm not sure he's good enough for Bec. Look at it this way – Rob is so serious-minded he makes accountants seen like crazy flag-burning radicals.

And before you start, no, I am not jealous. Rebecca and I were never that serious about one another, we were pals. Pals who slept together in college. Everyone sleeps with everyone in college, it doesn't mean anything. Right? And anyway, like I said, I've never been that into the idea of marriage. I lived with my parents for too long to believe in the perfect relationship which is how they are seen by the rest of the world. 'Forty years together and still loving every minute of it.' Oh, give me a break.

You don't need to know my parents to know their type. They give lifetime commitment a bad name. My folks make divorce an ideal to aspire to. I used to lie awake at night listening to them argue, wishing that they would just get normal and split up like everyone else's folks. But now I've started to think they actually like bickering. They have imaginatively turned pettiness into the cornerstone of their relationship. Forget fibre, they bicker to stay regular.

Anyway, Rob and Bec's decision to tie the knot has kind of given me pause. It seems that all my friends are getting hitched. There's only me and George left, unless you count Dave which you probably shouldn't given that he's gay, and anyway even he's got a Significant Other now compared to all the Insignificant Others of his past.

George, on the other hand, is just an asshole. I'm not being a jerk, he boasts about what a bastard he is himself. He tells girls before he sleeps with them that he's a bastard and that they shouldn't trust him. And you know what? They still sleep with him. He says it's because he poses a challenge.

But without sounding like Mr Ego, I'm not a bad guy. A few girls have even wanted to marry me. Nice girls, attractive girls, girls most guys would be happy to share a mortgage with. Maybe I'm just not the marrying kind. Disposable sex is still fine by me. I'll stick to tying knots in condoms. At least with a condom, when it's over it's over. They never try and talk a guy into one last time.

Anna stumbled into the Grill's restroom last night while I was taking a leak. Her first word was 'Woah!' Which was a great start from my point of view. I've been waiting for a girl to say 'Woah!' when I took my pants down all my life. What's more, she was a total babe. She was wearing this amazing gun-metal grey latex dress that looked like she might have sprayed it on, an unlit cigarette hanging off her lip, Brigitte Bardot-like, and a pair of cat's ears that made her look so cute I wanted to cuddle her on sight. It was ages before I realised I hadn't zipped up. She had to point it out in fact.

I don't believe in love at first sight, so don't get too carried away. There was a voice inside my head when I saw her, though, a voice I didn't recognise – a sort of crazy, boho Village Voice – that just kept telling me to go for it. 'Go for it man, what are you waiting for?' it urged.

'Do you know where you're going?' I asked awkwardly, taking her in with the sort of boyish concern that most girls seem to fall for.

She looked stumped and crinkled up her brow. 'Hey, that's not the sort of weighty issue you want to dive into when you're dying for a waz,' she replied, and then she just stood there staring at me weirdly like I was naked. Before telling me to zip up.

Generally speaking, I'm not a go-for-it kind of

guy. It's not something I'm proud of. I wish I was more go-get-it but I guess I'm just one of life's waiters. Growing up in Greenwich, Connecticut can do that to you. Maybe it's something in the water that predisposes a guy to caution. But last night I found myself listening to this Village Voice inside my head, and going for it.

Only maybe I should have thought more carefully about my chat-up line. That was where my plan was flawed, see. Stupidly, I asked her where she got her dress.

'My dress?' she looked at me suspiciously. 'Hang on, if I tell you, are you going to want to buy one or something? Because I hate it when people do that. I don't want to tell you if you're planning to look like me. It's very hard for a girl to maintain the integrity of the individual if everyone else starts dressing like her.'

I assured her that her individual integrity was safe with me.

'Well, anyway, I got it here,' she admitted.

I looked around the restroom, slightly bewildered. 'You can buy, like . . . clothes at the Grill?' I asked.

'Sorry, I meant in New York generally. Or isn't that specific enough for you? You want details, I guess? Receipts of purchase? Authenticity reports? Washing instructions?' She was laughing.

Talk about my finest hour. Not.

And that was where the portentous thing got a good grip. You have to understand this much: Anna was the opposite of every girl I've ever met. I can't imagine any of my previous girlfriends spraying their clothes on, or wearing cat's ears, or imagining that I might want them to share their fashion tips with me. We just clicked. It was as easy and as fast and as dangerous as that.

She was funny, loud, frank, and the best kisser I've ever met. 'Snogging', she called it. She'd been living in England with her father for years and had this really cool accent. Just listening to her made me want to hold her.

It wasn't until I woke up at her place and saw her mother's books that I realised who she is. As in *really* is. She's Anna Denier, daughter of Topsy Denier, the outrageous feminist who's always in the news. The sexy red-head who wrote all those wild books urging women to put down the scatter cushions and do whatever the hell they wanted.

My father bought *all* her books. He used to plant them strategically around the house in the hope my mother would read them one day and be inspired. Scatter cushions were the bane of my existence. We had to puff them up after we stood up and rearrange then in the artistic fan pattern so loved by my mother. Even today, my dad is still rearranging those cushions when he gets up. If he hadn't been an investment banker I think he would have devoted his life to the disarmament of scatter cushions.

Topsy Denier was the first unobtainable crush I ever had. Since then there have been too many to list, but Topsy was my first and as such a lasting favourite. I look up at Ernie and he smiles back as if approving my evolving plan. 'Maybe your teenage crush on Topsy could be the hook, buddy?' his grin seems to suggest.

'Good thinking Ernie,' I reply, giving him a conspiratorial wink. Then I check my teeth and gargle with mouthwash. 'I'll use Topsy as leverage to spread this thing with Anna over into another date – or beyond brunch at least.'

Ernie cackles his approval.

CHAPTER THREE

What do they do with all the fat they suck out of women's thighs every day? Recently, I've been unable to sleep at night as I ponder this issue. Sometimes I wake up in a cold sweat, screaming, 'Where is it all going?'

It has to go somewhere unless they are shipping it into outer space.

Are there mounds of it on the outskirts of LA? I wonder. And what is the likely environmental impact of the lipomountion? Is anyone even looking into this time bomb? Just when you start to get used to living with the breakdown of the ozone layer, fascist smoking laws and the latest breakdown in cervical smear tests, the lipomountain hits.

Dear Anna,
This is a great little piece. Although I think we need to soften it just a little, don't you? Perhaps a jokey aside to show you're not against surgical procedures when administered by a qualified practitioner?
Best wishes,
The Jerk (your editor)

Extract from the 'New York Girl' column of Anna Denier

Anna

When I stir back into consciousness again, I open one
tentative eye and observe The Count clock by my bed
click on to 2:06pm. Ouch!

The clicking noise as the five turns to six rever-
berates through my body like a colonic irrigation.
I'd toy with the idea of suicide only I don't have the
muscular control for anything as strenuous as death
right now. Maybe later, after a few handfuls of Advil
and a bucket of Alka Seltzer.

Binocular vision reveals a tray on the floor beside
my bed, on which there is an empty bottle of Krug
(Vintage).

PS: I have rarely drunk anything remotely like
vintage champagne in my life, and definitely never
in my own home. Are you kidding? A girl could take
her eye out with one of those corks. That's all I need
– a flat chest, an obsession with cereal and a glass
eye. Men will be throwing themselves off buildings
to get at me.

A glass bowl I vaguely recognise from my bathroom

cabinet contains, not the cotton buds I am familiar with, but the butt-ends of strawberries and smears of what at a sniff is revealed to be, erk, yoghurt. (V. good for intestinal tract harmony, Sienna tells me.)

On the floor beside this feast I spot a pile of sucked dry oyster shells and, most unpleasant of all, a used condom with a very professional reef knot tied in the end.

PS: I don't need to sniff any of this lot to recognise it for what it is. Ubergross.

But I'm a sick girl and so I study the detritus for some time, first with my left eye, then my right, and then in a brave move, both eyes simultaneously. I try and link it to my life, but there is a huge thudding noise my head. I want to believe that the champagne and oysters, not to mention the used condom, belong in my life, but I am a born cynic. I am also sweating heavily. I throw off the sheet and blow on my naked chest in a makeshift fan manoeuvre.

'Your whole life is makeshift!' I hear a voice inside me hiss.

I should have mentioned earlier that recently an Upper East Side girl has started cohabiting my distinctly downtown/West Village body. This girl wants things from my life and my body that I can never hope to give anyone in my current financial state. She has to face it, since moving to New York my bank account and my body are flaccid in a way that no amount of peppy health talks are going to change.

I point this out to my resident alien but she persists in her demands for weekends in the Hamptons, a gym with a roof pool, a career trajectory that she can discuss at cocktail parties, a pair of $400 shoes she saw in Barneys and charge cards that actually work. Yeah right, that's really going to happen.

Her demands make me feel v. inadequate, though. 'Everything about your life is falling apart,' she jeers when I do things like stuff panties down my bra to make myself look more womanly, or use nail-polish to disguise the holes in my tights.

I hate to make anyone homeless but this bitch has to go. I've already got the number of a reputable exorcist from Sienna. She's really handy with all that esoteric, spiritual new-age stuff. She's not so much a hippie as a very open being, she explained to me when we first met. She survives on a diet of German industrial music and herbal elixirs and blames everything, including the A-train, on past life karma. I've never met anyone like her. All my friends in London were really rational and would have screamed with laughter at the thought of exorcism or the Kabala, but now I take it all as perfectly normal. She's a very convincing person once you get past the purple turban.

The way I see it, Sienna is a girl that spends her life doing all the stuff the rest of us girls quite fancy doing but somehow never dare. You know, like travelling to the sorts of exotic places where antibiotics pass as currency, experimenting with drugs and snogging guys before she's been introduced. She can tell you everything you ever wanted to know about hallucinogenic mushrooms but were too afraid to ask. Sienna's been there done that. She's the sort of girl anyone would be happy to sit next to at a dinner party. I think she has a job but I'm not sure what it is, and that's another cool thing about New York – this is a city where a girl can have some mystery (even if she can't pay her rent or get laid).

I'd gladly swap my life for Sienna's if it weren't for the dearth of men in it. Despite wanting forevers, her relationships rarely go beyond that first snog, which I secretly blame on all the herbal elixirs containing garlic that she consumes. But what would I know?

She told me recently that she thinks I'm on a really high dose of karma and that's why I feel so dispirited. So now I'm trying to cut back. Part of my new low-karma diet includes not sending the e-mails I write to my editor, The Jerk. I'm also abstaining from sex with artists, students and aspirant authors.

Thinking about it, I suspect that the oysters, condom and champagne constitute a v. high-karma situation. I roll over and try to groan my way through the pain barrier of my body.

New York is a city where if you are not living on the edge, you are taking up too much space.'

I wrote this *Nike*-lifestyle statement on a bathroom wall when I first got here. A few weeks back, when I was a lot younger, more centred and definitely more arrogant. Before my mother's book came out, basically.

Ah yes ... my mother's book. Ah yes ... my mother. I'm sure you've heard of her, Topsy Denier? AKA chat-show-feminist and general reactionary-attention-seeking-champagne-swilling-nightmare? She talks about herself in the third person. Yes *that* Topsy – the eighties woman who put the sex into the sex wars.

And before you ask, yes, it's all true. Everything you've heard. She dipped my pacifiers in champagne, she dragged me to Studio 54 as a reward for getting an A in spelling bee in the third grade. My child-hood makes Saffy's in *Ab Fab* look unremarkable and suburban. Because on top of everything else, I had to endure all that dreary feminist junk. And believe me, it wasn't easy for a little girl being told at breakfast that my father's testicles belonged in the blender.

It wasn't easy on my father, Jack, either. That's why he moved to London. Topsy still lives in San Francisco (natch), although she is rarely there. Her life is one big 'I-can't-even-begin-to-tell-you-how-fabulous-my-life-is' book tour. However, I can tell you now, without need of reclaimed memory method, therapist or mind altering drugs, that I blame Topsy for all my problems.

I know that's a big call but someone's got to put their hand up for the way I turned out and it sure as hell isn't going to be me. I've got enough on my plate and besides, that's what parents are for aren't they, to sue and to loathe? I can't afford to go into litigation, so I've just settled for loathing.

Having Topsy for a mother gave me some strange views on life. 'Change your man before changing your perfume,' she used to tell me when we went out shopping. She also thought champagne was a cure-all for maladies from snakebite to toothache. No matter what the trouble, it was always, 'Soak it in Bolly, Eggnog.'

Eggnog is Topsy's nick-name for me. It's a term of endearment, a reference to my origins as an egg. Men say 'fruit of my loins', women say 'egg of my womb'. (Now you know how I suffer.)

My mother is obsessed with the egg issue. Why wouldn't she be? It's topical. Topsy loves topical. Once she got wind of this latest breakthrough in reproductive technology and worked out that girls can freeze their eggs – lay them down like good wines – there was no turning back. Good wines and a good cause? It was a custom-made issue for Topsy.

I can't switch on the television without seeing her now, prattling on about a woman's right to have it all . . . on the rocks! That's the name of her new book: *I'll Have Mine On The Rocks!*. It hit the New York bestseller list around the same time I hit New York.

It's not that I've got a problem with her subject matter. Far from it. I'm even considering putting my own eggs on ice for the future. It's like the sixteenth-century French philosopher Pascal's Just-In-Case theory on the existence of God. We don't know whether God exists or not, but as a gambler you're better off believing that he/she does. That way, if there is a God, you won't be embarrassed in the afterlife, and if there isn't, so what, you haven't lost anything.

I don't think I want kids but I'd like to go for the Just-In-Case option and set aside some eggs now. If I could afford to that is. Not that I'd tell Topsy I'm thinking of doing something she recommends. She'd have me on *Oprah* before I could say the words 'media-blitz'.

I blow on my chest some more. It is the first really hot New York morning of the year and it's only the end of April. How am I going to cope with July? Or August even? I've heard that people actually expire on the streets of New York in August and I have this fear of becoming one of these statistics.

I have a terror of dying alone, see. It just seems so, well . . . so lonely, really. I hate the thought that rats will feast on my remains for weeks before anyone finds me. I visualise the eternally youthful Topsy identifying my rat-chewed carcass. 'Yes, I recognise the hangnails on that chewed up hand!' she'll sigh melodramatically, as she signs photograph of herself for the detective in charge of the investigation.

The backs of my eyes feel as if the glue-ball that is my brain is leaking toxic poisons into them. I only returned to the land of my birth a few weeks ago and already the city that never sleeps has changed me. I arrived at JFK bright-eyed and ready for anything. That was back in the days when I was still innocent enough to think that scoring an apartment with a fireplace was a coup. The paper I write for arranged everything. I was offered a choice of air-conditioning on West End Ave. or a fireplace on Hudson.

Now I realise that I should have set my sights on air-conditioning – wherever it was. It is AC that gives you cred in this town. Who the hell has time for logs in the city that never sleeps?

I'd be lying if I said I left London without a fight. It wasn't really just a case of too many married friends. My boss there, who coincidentally is also known as The Jerk, decided it would be really neat, if I would, well . . . fuck off basically. I wrote a column for feisty single girls, 'Anna Denier Dishes', which he said was getting, and I quote, 'tired'.

Basically, our affair had come to an end. He had found a cuter younger, dumber girl to lavish his ravishings on. (Subtext: it was his penis that was tired, not my column.) And in all his crotch-induced wisdom he decided that it would be better to shove me in a city seven hours away by plane from my fans. He spoke to his buddy in New York (The New York Jerk), and got me this gig. They have a sort of transatlantic cast-off-affairs-exchange-program going from what I can gather.

I pull my face out of my pillow, just before suffocation takes full effect, and face once more the array of objects by my bed that have no place in my life. The truth is, I haven't had a sexual experience involving another person since I arrived in New York. I was starting to forget how to get condoms out of the packet.

I blow harder on my chest. When I do manage to

bring down some prey and get a man into my bed, it usually ends in an unsatisfactory climax, like him saying he has to go home to feed his cat or me sending him out for cigarettes and then not answering the intercom when he buzzes.

At least that was my life in London. Here in New York I hadn't so much as met any prey. Everybody with one head, a job and no kids in New York is gay. There'll be a lot of books and documentaries on the subject later on next summer. I know this for a fact because I'll be the girl writing them.

I push my face back into my pillow and wonder whether it's worth getting up and going out for the papers. Maybe I should struggle into the new, barely-there dress by Stella McCartney. The one my editor bought me as a fuck off present. It's hanging on the back of the door, practically begging me to go downstairs to Nadine's for brunch. I stick on a pair of dark sunglasses and jam a Camel on my lower lip while I consider this option. And that's when he walks in. The God-Boy. Woah!

CHAPTER FOUR

My daughter doesn't take my calls, or if she does, I can't help feeling it was an accident. She forgot to call-screen or something.

That's daughters. You give birth, you feed, adore and care for them, live for their happiness, dilute your own dreams so theirs might be enriched. Whatever you do, they grow up to resent you. And that's what I really resent – my daughter's resentment.

The worst part is not being able to put my finger on what it is that I did so wrong. Was it because I divorced her irrepressibly unfaithful father? Was it because I was a public campaigner for the rights of women? Did she feel that she grew up in the shadow of a movement directed towards improving her future and the future of all women? She rolls her eyes when I suggest these possibilities.

She claims it's because I breast fed her for too long.

Extract from *One True Love* by Topsy Denier

Anna

The guy standing before me towelling himself down and wearing my sarong is not just any guy, but the sort that belongs in a vitrine in a SoHo gallery.

Although not known for my gawking skills, I gawk now. And blink. And then gawk some more as my prey from the night before slumps onto the bed beside me and flicks cold drips of water over my face.

He's looking at me strangely, which isn't that surprising really. He probably thinks I'm about to have an epileptic episode. It takes me a minute before I realise that I am wearing:

1) dark sunglasses in bed,
2) trademark unlit cigarette on lower lip,
3) nothing else.

Another Ubercool look from Anna Denier.

'Hot or what?' he announces. (I think he's referring to the weather rather than me.)

Guys in my flat the 'morning after' are not something I normally do, so I'm kind of stuck for the up-beat response he's eagerly expecting. Sometimes

I might stay overnight at a guy's place, but that's another matter. This is my retreat, my Girl Zone, my *sanctum sanctorum* with its pile of dolls and soft toys from my childhood propped up on the sofa like a disapproving audience. If anything, this is the place where I seek passive respite from men and their kind.

Men only ever enter the Girl Zone for the purpose of a thrashing under the sheets. Sheets, moreover, changed straight after said man leaves to either feed his cat or fetch me cigarettes. Always before sleep time, though. And here lies my problem. This guy before me now is not a man in the normal sense of the word. He's a fantasy guy.

He is still rubbing himself down with the towel. 'Man, is it hot?' he repeats. I am ogling him so hard my eyes hurt; they have started opening and closing in a sort of wide-awake REM as the night before comes back to me. He's not my usual type. Too good looking, too much sex appeal and, thanks to my shower facilities, too bloody clean. I can't even remember his name. I hear the regret-squad marching towards me in their jack boots as the previous night's events reveal themselves like a slide show.

Slide one: The Tribeca Grill with The Jerk (welcome to New York drink).

CUT TO:

Slide two: Margaritas (three).

CUT TO:

Slide 3: Blonde waitress noticing my cool, unlit Camel on lower lip tells me I can't smoke (like I hadn't worked that out yet).

CUT TO:

Slide 4: On finding out I'm related to the famous Topsy-*I'll-Have-Mine-On-The-Rocks!*-Denier (thanks to The Jerk), she asks for my autograph. Uber, uber, uberembarrassing.

CUT TO:

Slide 5: Me blushing, about to cry with embarrassment.

CUT TO:

Slide 6: Me running aimlessly into the men's restroom.

CUT TO:

Slide 7: Sexy guy at latrine, hair to die for (well, technically not much hair, but buzz-cut to die for). Not to mention nice bone structure, clear skin and etceteras. Loads of etceteras.

CUT TO:

Slide 8: Medium to heavy flirtation, as much as possible given the circumstances (i.e. other bloke in toilet cubicle throwing up).

CUT TO:

Slide 9: Sexy guy at latrine smuggling me out of Tribeca Grill away from The Jerk and taking me to a club he knew in the East Village. V. much the IT place he told me.
CUT TO:
Slide 10: Dancing.
CUT TO:
Slide 11: Further drinking.
CUT TO:
Slide 12: Further flirting.
CUT TO:
Slide 13: Further dancing.
CUT TO:
Slide 14: Sexy guy at latrine hailing cab (I remember being impressed as he fought off another less-deserving couple who claimed that it was their cab).

I still can't remember where the oysters and champagne came into the equation, and I don't even want to imagine what the yoghurt was all about, but I do remember kissing sexy guy at latrine's face off in the cab. After that, well . . . it's all a bit unclear again. Evidence suggests, though, that we must have ended up at my place, in my bed and gone, well . . . all the way really.
Whoops.

Clearly he hasn't a cat to go home and feed and I must have fallen asleep before sending him out on the obligatory cigarette run because Mark (I remember his name now) is still here. In my flat. Availing himself of my amenities (such as they are). And this is not good. Not good at all. I try hard to convince myself of that principle.

'Hot or what?' he repeats for a third time.

I wish he'd stop saying that. What else can it be other than hot? It must be one hundred degrees if it's ten. But then all media attorneys have a habit with rhetoric and I remember now that this is what he told me he did for a living. Although significantly, in the few hours I have spent in this guy's company, he hasn't told me that much about himself, which is strange. My standard prey like to tell all in the first night. Fill my brain up with their stories, only to disappear, leaving me to do the DELETE.

'Hangover huh?' he inquires solicitously. It is at this point that I notice that I'm dribbling. He is undeniably yummy. I don't just mean hot either, I mean sweaty. Until he speaks.

'Your mother wrote that egg book, right?'

This is very bad as far as opening gambits go. The worst really. Like the Girl Zone, the Topsy Zone should be avoided by all one night stands. I groan.

That was the best part about living in London. No one knew about Topsy.

'Cool lady or what?' he continues, oblivious to the emotional minefield he is traversing.

I grin back at him insanely. I wonder if it's physically possible to stick your own hand down your throat and drag out your internal organs.

'Wasn't she an eco-feminist a few years back?'

'Huh?' I grunt. (Because I'm very eloquent in the morning and I'm trying to impress.)

'An eco-feminist, anti-medical interventionism in the womb? I've read all her books. *Get The Hell Out Of My Womb* came out the day I lost my virginity.' He laughs, looking at me as if I should join him.

Somehow, I muster the capability to reply. 'That must have been, um . . .'

He nods. 'Amazing? Yeah, sure was.' He starts picking up my dolls and checking them out as he speaks. No man has ever touched my Barbie before. She's the one with the biggest breasts ever. Ultimate Barbie's her name, limited edition. She is so cool. Even Sienna is into Ultimate Barbie. Who wouldn't be? She's got it all; too much, according to some. The ultimate Power Babe. But this doll is not for touching.

My eyes tumble out of my face like caviar spilling from a bowl at the shock of seeing a guy defile her.

He's making her arms and legs move in a v. crude fashion. It's, it's, it's . . . appalling. But he appears not to notice how outraged I am as he outlines his feelings for Topsy. 'Huge. Totally huge. Can you imagine, the day I lost my virginity?' He's looking at Barbie as he asks this.

'The day you lost your virginity. Let me think back. No, no I can't, sorry. Not in detail,' I respond, amazed at my own savvy, but again he doesn't seem to hear me. His looks up at my light fitting, a musical mobile from my nursery, depicting, who else, Old Mother Hubbard.

'Yeah, I remember the cover vividly. She was a bit of a pin-up for a lot of us guys at Harvard.'

I am confused. 'Who, the girl you did it with?'

'Your mother.'

This is very, very wrong. 'You want me, her daughter, to picture you, the guy I just slept with, fantasising about my mother? That's . . . that's . . . that's . . .'

He looks crestfallen. 'I guess you don't want to hear that do you?'

'No,' I state firmly, but I don't want to go to that place right now. Mark is too, too cute. In fact, thinking about it, he can't really be straight. Maybe last night was an aberration. Or maybe he's bi, it's very cool now to be bi. For starters, he just said that he went to Harvard which I always thought was a

43

key-code for 'I'm gay'. Then there is his body, his butt and his smile. And it is definitely the body, the butt and the smile of a gay guy.

The mayor of New York passed a law on it a few years back, I think. Only ugly, emotionally dysfunctional guys with messy divorces in their past get to be straight in New York.

'I guess you don't want to hear that the guy you just slept with used to fantasise about your mother. I guess that was a totally dumb thing to say. Sorry.' He slaps his forehead.

'Fantasise,' I repeat the word, rolling it around my pounding head like a worry bead. I can't associate the word with Topsy. I just can't. okay, so she's not bad looking, but how can any man fantasise about a woman who wants to liquidise another man's testicles in her kitchen appliances?

I try and imagine his dreamy eyes fantasising about my mother. I stun-gun this image, though, and chase it from my imagination. I only want his eyes fantasising about me. This guy is good looking enough to collect DNA samples off, and I have an urge to do so right this moment. With my tongue.

'It must be so cool to have a mother like that,' he sighs, leaning back on Big Ted.

I jerk into a sitting position. 'Let me get this straight, my mother is cool because . . . why exactly?'

He chuckles, ignoring the edge to my voice. 'Hey, you should meet my mother. I can't imagine her even reading about the stuff your mom writes about. She is so *not* into women's rights. Connecticut ladies sticking their eggs on ice?' He shakes Barbie's head. 'No way. That is not going to happen, ever. My mother and sex is *never* going to happen.'

'Well, your mother and sex must have happened at least once,' I point out, as if I'm his biology teacher. 'Otherwise you wouldn't exist.' And then it hits me! But of course. He doesn't exist, he is my fantasy guy. I try and remember if I have a camera handy. A Polaroid, ideally. 'Has anyone ever taken a photograph of you?' I inquire lightly. 'Or captured your image on video? In fact, now that we're on the subject, do you even have a shadow?'

He laughs. 'You're so wild.' He puts his hands around my face, puckering up my lips and cheeks into a look I know can't be flattering. Then he kisses me. He tastes of toothpaste. I am almost certain that I taste of cigarettes and old oysters.

'And much better looking than your mother,' he adds, before going in for the full mushy, 'That was so cool last night. Wasn't it cool?' Then he pulls away to study my puckered face. It's a great look (not).

I can still feel his lips on mine as I nod. I can't quite believe that I have managed to drag home an actual

God-Boy. God-Boys are not normally my style. I ogle them, sure, but young, hunky, successful rich guys are not for the likes of me, a normal, neurotic girl of erratic income, with a fondness for cereal, decreasing enthusiasms and increasing cynicisms. I go for older married men or very broke artistic types who live in lofts and sleep on futons and don't bother washing their underwear or anything as anal as that. That way they don't expect too much and neither do I. I write failure into my relationships before I get too attached. It's my equivalent to a prenuptial.

But I am feeling stirrings inside me that don't sit well with my usual, just-woken-up-with-a-stranger schedule. I notice that his mouth is moving again. Noise is coming out. I try to pay attention. 'My sister sexed her foetuses,' he is telling me. 'You know, to make sure she was having a girl? Said she didn't want a kid with a penis. Said it irked her, the whole idea of a Bris.'

'A Bris?'

'Removal of the foreskin. You know, Rabbis, relatives, light refreshments? As a mother she finds it cruel and demeaning, doing that to a baby. My sister hates blood.'

'Well, see here's a thought. You can leave foreskins on you know. It has been done,' I inform him.

'Not in my family,' he assures me. 'We haven't had foreskins in my family for thousands of years.'

This strangely impresses me. I couldn't even tell you what my ancestors were doing two generations ago. 'Wow!' I say. 'That is a really, really long time.'

He grins. 'Yeah, it's almost an obsession with us.'

'That's amazing. I mean, you'd think they'd realise they weren't wanted and stop growing. Like appendixes and that prehensile tail thing we used to have when we lived in trees.'

He starts falling about with laughter which is, like, sooo gratifying. It makes me glow.

'Seriously, though, what a cool mom. It must have been great for you as a kid having a mother like Topsy, giving you all that positive affirmation. My mother was so into repressing our natural urges, it hurt just being in the same room with her sometimes.'

'Oh, you'd be surprised,' I tell him in my glibber than glib tone. But he doesn't seem to hear.

'I mean, we even had to puff up the cushions every time we got off the couches in the TV room. Can you imagine how embarrassing that was? When the guys came over to watch a ball game and you had to ask them to puff their cushions?'

I have to admit that his personal experiences with his mother in the teen-embarrassment-zone are alien to me. My teen-embarrassment-zone involved my mother quizzing guys about their interest in the female orgasm. This was a big factor in deciding to live with my father, actually.

'She still has my dad pumping up those cushions,' he adds, shaking his head.

I try to imagine my own father pumping up cushions, but it's too far-fetched. My father wouldn't recognise a cushion unless it was implanted in a woman's breast. Plus, it's hard to imagine anything other than the feel of Mark's cheeks on mine right now.

PS: He has the clearest skin I have ever seen.

'So, are you going for it?' he asks, just as I am about to melt into his arms and break my no-sex-in-the-morning rule. I don't know what he is talking about, but I suspect he is about to kick me out of the I'll-do-anything-for-another-one-of-your-kisses zone.

'What?' I ask, holding the sheet against my chest, (as if I have anything to hide).

'Sticking your eggs on ice so you don't have to deal with that biological clock ticking shit? Man, that must be a drag.' He sits on the bed and arches his back so that I can count his stomach muscles. He is brown and deliciously scrubbed looking, like guys used to look on cigarette commercials – when they still had cigarette commercials.

'Do you hear me ticking or something?' I say, only

half joking. I really don't want to discuss kids with anyone at the moment – and certainly not with a guy I only dragged home last night. That would be the saddest thing I've ever done and that is a really, really long list. And anyway, it's probably a test he does on all the girls he sleeps with just to find out how needy and clucky they are. But I'm not falling for the bait. I don't miss a beat. 'I haven't got time for biology,' I explain lightly. 'I don't even eat salad.'

He looks amazed.

'No, really,' I insist. 'My life is one long stream of openings, parties and waking up alone in the Girl Zone, or on rare occasions in the lofts of poor artistic guys with delusions of their own coolness. There's absolutely nothing ticking inside Anna Denier. I practise safe sex and mean it okay, so you've got nothing to worry about with me.'

He is grinning. 'I wasn't.'

I feel so dumb. I drop the sheet and fold my arms across my chest, giving myself an artificial cleavage. Normally I wear my bra to bed, but . . . well, I guess a lot of habits were broken last night. I must look pretty gruesome. I can only imagine that my hair's on end, my mascara's smeared in Gothic rings and my lipstick's kissed into a clownish grin.

'Girl Zone hey?' Mark flings the towel he was drying his hair with over the back of a chair. 'I guess I've made you pissed. First I talk about my fantasies about your mother and then I start going on about your biological clock. You and your mother probably have a good laugh about the dumb stuff guys say and do?'

This guy could give button-pushing lessons at Columbia. 'News flash,' I snap. 'My mother and I have never had a good laugh about anything. Apart from our gender we are as different as, well . . . any different stuff you care to name.'

'Chalk and cheese?' he suggests.

'Good and evil,' I argue. 'My mother is a champagne-swilling eighties nutter with an endless appetite for chat-show revelations. Whereas I am a cigarette-sucking, new millennium blonde (for the last month anyway), with no political manifesto to speak of and a pronounced hatred of chat-shows.'

He nods and shrugs his shoulders as if I'm splitting the atom over the difference between my mother and me. He has an athlete's shoulders. I bet he works out at a gym on one of those rowing machines that make a swishing sound. He probably even owns one and works out night and day.

I regret mouthing off and decide to soften the blow of the inevitable good-bye speech in which he will do a guy line. Like saying he will call when he knows he won't. I will do a girl thing like believing him.

Already the thought of not gazing upon his beauty

forever scares me. But I know that it is inevitable. I want to put him on a podium or in a glass display case and look at him forever, like a Duchampian exhibit or a fragment of the Magna Carta.

'Shit, did I leave this here?' he asks suddenly, breaking my reverie. He is standing before me, looking almost shocked, almost ashamed, holding the used condom between his finger and thumb with a great show of disbelief.

I nod.

He grimaces, horrified. 'Am I a pig or what?'

I wait a beat before replying, just in case he has an alternative term for men who dump their condoms by the bed after intercourse. He looks lost, so I help him out. 'Of course you are,' I assure him. 'You're a guy aren't you?'

I hate myself immediately. It sounds like a snippet of dialogue my mother might have used on the Rosie O'Donnell show. I hate all that male/female, girl-power/ladism, gender disparity shit that dominated my childhood. I'm turning into my mother.

It is while contemplating this attack on his gender that Mark does something he probably should have put off till later, i.e. after I'd had a few Advils and an Alka Seltzer. He takes off the sarong to expose his erection. Unfortunately, he does this at the exact moment my stomach loses the battle over nausea and I heave.

CHAPTER FIVE

I've been assured by friends that the ultimate in intimacy is watching your lover shave while you take a pee. Which more or less explains why one in three marriages ends in divorce.

I've read Men Are From Mars, Women Are From Venus, *but as far as I'm concerned couples come from another galaxy altogether.*

Extract from the 'New York Girl' column of Anna Denier

Anna

Talk about bad timing. I wish more than anything that I could transmogrify into any other girl on the planet (but preferably one with a larger cup size than AA). I haven't actually barfed in the true sense of the US vernacular. There was no mess, just a loud, hollow, nauseous sound. More a burf than a barf, really. Yes, that's all it was, a burf, somewhere between a burp and a barf.

Just the same, Mark seems decidedly demoralised. Actually, he looks destroyed. Barf or burf, it came out sounding personal. 'Your dick makes me want to throw up,' it declared. God I feel awful, not to mention mean and senselessly cruel, as I watch him carefully scrutinising every inch of his genitals for the kind of grotesque growth that could have triggered my gross-out.

I will myself to say something that might reassure him, but I am too—? Too what? Embarrassed? Ashamed? Unworthy of a life support system should I fall into a coma? Pond-scum like? None of these terms comes even close. Actually, I need a new term, a whole dictionary of new terms for the way I feel. Unfortunately, the very term exists for the colour I've turned. Puce.

My neighbour's stereo is pumping out an old Prodigy hit which I used to love, but the lyrics aren't helping my sense of innate pointlessness now. 'Smack My Bitch Up', the singer orders. 'Smack My Bitch Up!'

Meanwhile, Mark's erection has deflated like a punctured inner tire. I have just barfed (or burfed) at what many Freudians out there deem to be a man's very sense of self.

I close my eyes and wish I'd read Sienna's copy of *Personal Majick for the Novice* more carefully. Especially the part that explained how to rub your body with a home-made mustard that renders you invisible. Sienna swears by it, especially when the landlord comes banging on her door for the rent.

Look at the poor guy. I doubt he'll have another erection in his life. My mother couldn't have achieved this level of male humiliation with all the kitchen appliances in the world. Mark's manhood lolls miserably between his legs. He looks at me. I look at him. He looks at it, hanging there limp and useless.

I have to face it, I am something I never wanted to be: a metaphorical castrater of men. A Bobbittor to rival Topsy. I've always had a formidable reputation for saying the wrong things to the wrong people at the wrong time, but this is a new low, even for me.

'I wasn't retching because of your penis,' I try and explain. 'I mean, I honestly feel queasy . . . honestly.' The pervasive smell of old oyster shells and the talk of ova, not to mention my mother, have taken their toll, I tell him. But Mark is deaf to all my entreaties.

'Talk about not being a sex-in-the-morning sort of girl,' I joke as lightly as the circumstances allow.

He doesn't acknowledge me. So, stupidly, I carry on. When I'm in a hole I love to keep digging in the hope I'll find treasure. 'Why is it, do you think, that men love sex in the morning and girls don't?' I ask him, as if we were back in the loo at the Tribeca Grill tossing round theories on twenty-first century existence.

He looks at me like one of those really cool, hip, artistic types who smoke roll-ups and hang out on the edge of what it means to be sane. You know, the guys who have shorter-than-short attention spans and practically live in those ubercool bars in Alphabet City. A look that seems to be tossing up the virtues of murder and suicide.

'Talk about mismatched biorhythms,' I mutter, shrugging matter of factly, in the misguided hope that he'll shrug with me. I think that's a saying, actually – Shrug and the world shrugs with you. Point and you point alone.

Maybe not.

Anyway, Mark doesn't shrug. He goes back to searching his testicle sac as if he's expecting to find a weeping boil or a canker lurking on the underside. Watching him turn his equipment upside down that way makes me feel queasy again. I grimace. He catches my off-screen look out of the corner of his eye. Brilliant Anna, utterly, bloody, brilliant. Really destroy the guy why don't you.

He looks clinically depressed as he abandons his groin as beyond hope and listlessly wraps the sarong back around his perfectly tanned and toned torso.

He'll probably need professional help now. Just my luck. I wouldn't be surprised if his therapist encourages him to sue for sexual-ego damage. Which is scary. I mean, what can serious ego damage be worth in an age where men are prepared to pay the earth for one Viagra-induced erection?

Quite a lot, I imagine.

'It's nothing to do with your penis,' I repeat. 'Which by the way looked very . . . well . . . very . . . appealing,' I add uselessly.

He backs towards the door. And no wonder.

Appealing? Did I, diva of the adjective, say his

penis looked 'appealing'? I wish I could just strangle myself with my Wonderbra, I really do.

That's a point, where is my bra? A girl is nothing without a bra, or at least a cleavage, and in my case I need one to have the other. I start feeling about the bed but my movements startle him.

He's probably worried that I'm after a weapon because he starts gathering up his clothes and backing out of the room, apologising profusely for getting the wrong idea.

'Will you stop apologising?' I shout louder than I mean to. My nerves are on edge. 'Please don't say sorry anymore. I'm the one saying sorry. Here, listen to this. S-O-R-R-Y! I told you, it wasn't anything to do with you. It was just a barf that's all, an innocent, albeit unpleasant-sounding barf. Caused by a night of excess and a hangover. Definitely not your thing.'

'Thing?'

'Your penis, and besides, it wasn't even really a barf at all. It was more of a burf than a barf.'

'A burf?' he repeats dubiously.

'Something between a barf and a burp,' I explain, trying to sound all technical and knowing. 'They're . . . very . . . er . . . much the thing in London, actually. Hugely hip is burfing. Very cool in the club scene.'

He doesn't look convinced.

'Honestly, *Time Out* did a huge spread on great

burfers of Shoreditch only last year. I was just trying to cut you into the loop.' I feel my nose to see if it's growing.

'I see,' he mutters, but I can see he doesn't. He doesn't get burfing at all. It's a lost cause. I throw my hands in the air in despair. 'Why are men so obsessed with their dicks? I mean, why has everything got to revolve around your penis, huh? Can't a girl barf without you thinking it's about your genitals?'

'I thought you said it was a burf?' he reminds me, studying my face carefully. Probably to see if I'm on drugs. My editor looked at me like that when he took me for my welcome-to-the-Big-Apple dinner last night.

'Men just focus on their dicks too much,' I continue, as if I'm some sort of huge authority on the subject. 'You should be more like me. Body oblivious.'

'Body oblivious?'

'It's true, I could happily give myself a hysterectomy right now, here, on this bed,' I assure him. 'And my ego wouldn't suffer in the least.'

I start humming along to the repeat playing of 'Smack My Bitch Up'. Mark looks like he's wondering how fast he can get dressed and get out of my neighbourhood.

'You guys are really something. It's as if your penis is a super-ego. A manifestation of who you are. Which is really silly when you think about it.'

'Silly?' he repeats. I wish he would stop doing that, scrutinising all the dumb stuff I say. Cause it really bothers me. Why can't he just idolise my nutty way with language, the way my readers do?

I sit still and try and shut up, wishing I was more like Samantha in *Bewitched* practising her witch-craft on the ill-equipped Darren. I wiggle my nose hopefully.

'Are you about to sneeze or something? he asks, taking another step back.

'No, I was just ... trying something.' I smile hopefully.

He looks at me stretched out on my bed. It's a fantasy arrangement of mattresses piled one on top of another. And yes, there is a pea at the bottom. I'm hoping that one day I'll find it and turn into a princess capable of whisking myself off on my shining platinum charge card.

'Seriously? You never think of your womb as part of who you are?' he questions me, finally entering into the spirit of the debate.

I shake my head emphatically. 'Never.' Just then my toe discovers my Wonderbra, tangled up in my tights at the end of the bed, and I dive down to retrieve it. I can hear him shuffling around as I struggle to get into it. Not used to putting a bra *on* in front of a guy, I do up the hooks with all the elegant grace of a beached octopus.

I love my Wonderbra. I've tried La Perla and just about every Italian lacy contraption designed to ruin a decent paycheque, but nothing gives me a cleavage like Wonderbra. It makes me feel like one of those girls with, well, with breasts really.

When I re-emerge, though, complete with confidence-inducing cleavage, Mark is getting dressed, which really, really, really isn't what I'm after. Bugger. Bugger. Bitch. Bum. Moments ago he was in the mood to ravish me, now, just as I relocate my wonder, he's off. Good one Anna. Absolutely bloody brilliant! Shag! Shit! Ass!

'What about your obsession with your eggs then?' he suddenly blurts as he pushes a long leg (I'd much rather was wrapped around me) into his Calvin's. I like the way they cling to his butt.

If I was of sane mind I'd tell him as much. I would look at him tantalisingly, perhaps even pout, and show him by my body language that I want to make up for my gross *faux pas* of earlier. Like I said, *if*. But sadly, given my mother, eggs are somewhat of a nuclear trigger issue with me.

I throw off my Little Miss Muffet sheet. '*My* obsession? *Hello*! You were the one who had the thousand and one questions about my egg-bank a minute ago.'

What the hell am I doing? I ask myself as soon as the words are out of my mouth. This time, I don't even wait to view the damage. I dive under the sheet and hope against hope that there will be some of that disappearing mustard stuff lurking down there in my tights.

But, amazingly, Mark replies in a normal tone of voice, as if he's really interested in the debate of penis-versus-womb obsession. 'What . . . you honestly never talk about stuff like that with your girlfriends? You must mention it *occasionally*,' he presses. 'With other girls, when there are no guys around? Com'n you must.'

I peek out, holding the sheet just below my eyes in case I have to dive for shame again. 'Well, hardly ever. Anyway, girls certainly never compare the size of their wombs,' I point out, as if this proves our superiority.

'Yes, but girls have breast envy.'

I wince. He's got me there. 'I don't know why I come out with this stuff. It just pours out of me like bile out of that little kid in *The Exorcist*.'

He pulls the boxers off again and comes towards me, softened by my little girl eyes and my irresistible vulnerability.

'I'm not very good in the morning at the best of times,' I apologise, feeling myself blush yet again.

He looks at the clock. 'What do you mean, the morning? It's after two in the afternoon. What time do you start having sex in Anna-land then?'

I make some desperate gabbled noises which I hope he'll interpret as 'Now, this second'!

But he doesn't. 'So, no sex, but let me take you out to breakfast. I know I'm starving.'

Food is the last thing on my mind. I suddenly want to take back all that guff about not being a sex-in-the-morning sort of girl and ravish and be ravished with the best of them.

'If you want you can help yourself to the contents of my kitchen,' I suggest, hoping that he'll disappear long enough for me to run a comb through my hair and a toothbrush through my mouth. 'Then you can come back to bed and we can do, you know, stuff,' I offer, placing a heavy emphasis on the word 'stuff'. I flutter my eyelashes but due to my standard overapplication of mascara, the left eyelash gets stuck to my cheekbone and rather spoils the effect.

'What contents? I checked out the refrigerator before I took a shower. Hey, what are you trying to breed in that kitchen of yours, E-coli?'

I face him, stunned. He's been in my kitchen already? I squash my face into my pillow. Now it really is over. I knew he was too good to be true, too good to be my type. Now he's seen the horror of my kitchen it's inevitable that he will flee. I almost want him to flee, just so I can start the healing process and get over him.

'Hey, you got a serious hangover or something?' he asks, pulling the hair from around the back of my neck.

'Yeah, something like that.'

'Shift your reality principle,' he urges, shoving me over so that he can scramble under the sheet and spoon himself against my body. I wriggle away, partly because of the heat, but mainly because I am already preparing myself for loss.

He huddles closer. Then he does something so uberdivine, I realise that I was right all along. He isn't real, he is an angel. I couldn't have conjured up a better guy if I had watched a squillion episodes of *Bewitched* and read a thousand books on Kabalistic spells.

He plants a wet kiss on my neck. Then he blows the wet kiss.

Then he plants another wet kiss further down and blows on that.

Then he does it again.

Then again and again, until I begin to purr.

It feels like I am being rubbed down with an ice

cube and I moan as all my nerve endings shoot down to my clitoris. Suddenly, I do feel like a sex-in-the-morning girl. Suddenly, I want nothing but sex, sex, sex.

But we don't have sex, we make love. Slowly, with a lot of long kissing, first on one end of the bed and then on the other, me on top, him on top, and Barbie underneath us both (for a moment I thought it was the pea).

I forget the heat and the fact that he's not real, and drown out the thumping base of Prodigy from the guy's stereo opposite with my own cries of pleasure. It's the coolest sex ever. But he is a fantasy-guy, a God-Boy, I remind myself, as he goes out later to get the papers and some Alka Seltzer. And God-Boys never come back. Once he is out that front door, he will remember that he does have a cat after all. Or a wife. Or a kingdom to rule over.

Just in case, I shower and make myself look as gorgeous as I possibly can, making the most of my long, long legs and my flat, flat chest. I get out my favourite snow-white Wonderbra (both cups of wonder intact) and team it with the low-cut, pale-as-snowdrops Stella McCartney. Then I twist my rat's nest of hair up and stick in a pencil to hold it in place. Even knowing that I am destined to be dropped from a great height can't make me wipe the smile from my face. I feel so good, I even find myself singing along to The Prodigy. It's the sort of music my mother has led protests over to ban

My soft toys and dolls shake their heads and sigh.

CHAPTER SIX

Sisterhood is a blurred concept. Theoretically, as girls we face similar stuff, but the truth is we are a bunch of desperate carnivores on the hunt for a limited amount of prey. And these days, with the herd numbers diminishing, we are forced to be more ruthlessly competitive than ever.

Women as sisters was a nice ideal for our mothers' generation, but gender identification is not that strong a bond in the race to find a partner in Manhattan. Put simply, other women are your worst enemies, unless they are fatter, older, or possess more chin hairs than you.

Extract from the 'New York Girl' column of Anna Denier

Mark

If a guy has something he doesn't want to talk about, a secret say, and someone finds out what that something is, he'll just explain it away by saying he forgot to mention it. We do it all the time. Ask any guy.

Girls, on the other hand, think of this behaviour as concealing vital information, or in some instances, telling a lie. How can not saying something be telling a lie? Clinton aside, okay?

Anna is quite clear on this point of not talking about stuff and lying. In fact, we've talked around the topic of secrets and lies a fair bit lately, while I've been trying to evaluate how much I should conceal in this relationship before I'm deemed to be lying. At this stage, I'm playing my cards close to my chest.

I used to play a lot of poker. I learnt it on the kibbutz in Israel. We would play cards at night, talk, joke around and smoke pot (inhaling, natch). I did a lot of stuff on that kibbutz that I've never done before. Losing my virginity for one.

'Shit,' I declare, looking down. 'I think I've lost

another button on my shirt.' Third one this month. In the few months I've been seeing Anna, I've lost a lot of buttons. It started with a Woah! and almost ended with a barf – or a burf, depending on which side of the pond you're from, apparently. But I'm still here.

Not officially, though; we still haven't had That Conversation. But I leave a toothbrush.

I'm sitting on the toilet in her tiny apartment in the Village. I sit here quite a lot. Anna says, if I become famous, her loo could become a shrine and push her rent up.

Seriously, though, I like the Village, or Underneath The Arches, as Anna calls it. Apparently it is the title of a living sculpture by Gilbert and George. See, that's the sort of stuff she knows. I love this neighbourhood, with its big city trends and its village vibe. I even like the noise, which is not inconsequential. The thumping music in the flat opposite Anna's is giving me tinnitus, I'm sure of it. I get this clicking noise at night when I'm trying to get to sleep.

Most of all I love the chaotic nursery atmosphere of Anna's apartment and the way she lives; never eating in, the shoe collection stacked on wall-to-floor racks, every surface covered in toys, never any reception on the television, and the entertaining slide show of screen saves on her computer which is always on, glowing in the corner like a nerve centre.

I'm pretty sure that I am in love with Anna. I've told her as much without stringing the words together in the traditional I Love You order. I can't be sure but I'm almost certain that she's fallen in love with me, although she assures me I'll hear the thud if she does. Maybe she's right and it's too soon to talk of love, but she lets me watch her shave her legs which has got to be pretty huge as far as intimacy goes, right?

We also have our own song: 'Smack My Bitch Up' (the guy in the flat opposite was playing it all the time when we first hooked up).

Our own drink: Manhattans, without ice (Anna's British influence).

Our own restaurants (so sad and limiting to have only one): Nadine's for brunch, otherwise Mercers Kitchen and Bowery Bar for people watching.

I love showing Anna around New York and listening to her talk about London. I guess she makes me look at things in a way I've never done before. Noticing things I've never noticed before. Smells, for example. I smell her on my clothes during the day when I'm at work; not her perfume you understand, but her. Something between vanilla and heaven.

Plus things have changed. The way I live my life has changed. The things I care about have changed.

I don't dare ask Anna if it's the same for her. Maybe it isn't. At work, I ring her whenever I get the chance, just to hear her voice. Also, I've stopped flirting with the new partner and wearing clothes that are obviously designer. The first time I wore my Gucci belt we were on the subway. She told me I should just carry a neon Gucci sign so that people everywhere could know of my devoted allegiance.

The real evidence that I am in love comes from my mother's behaviour. She's started telling me that I'm too young for a serious relationship. Which is a huge change for a woman who's been at me for the last year to meet a nice girl and settle down. I think she probably senses that Anna is a loose cannon in the field of cushion plumping.

My father adores her. He thinks Mom's worried that Anna might be a seditious influence on her rule of chintz. Which is probably true.

'Do you think Dome Head shaves his head to be cool or because he's balding and too shy to wear a toupee?' Anna asks idly, as she soaps her long legs in the bath.

Dome Head is Anna's name for my friend, George. She has nick-names for all my friends. Everyone joins the cast of *Sesame Street* when they meet Anna. I'm God-Boy and her editor is The Jerk. I've started thinking up names for people on the subway to pass the time, but Anna says that I have to give it up. She says I'm appropriating her personality.

I always talk about my friends disloyally with her and laugh about the stuff they say and do. Stuff I've always found funny or irritating, but never discussed with anyone outside our group. 'Toupee chicken, definitely,' I decide, after weighing Dome Head's baldness, and we laugh.

We laugh all the time. Even when we're making love. My friends don't trust Anna, though. They warn me about her in whispered, urgent tones, as if she is a gram of heroin in a seedy alley, and they're about to report me to the police. I am in grave danger of being busted.

'She's . . .,' they fumble, their lips pulled tightly together as if they've tasted something bitter.

'She's what?' I challenge.

'She's, just . . . well, she strikes me as dangerous.'

'Dangerous?'

'Not dangerous exactly. I mean, I know you can handle yourself buddy, but, well, frankly she's not . . . you.'

So there we have it. Anna is not me.

Which is not only a dumb thing to say but it makes me angry because what they're really saying is that she's not *us*. Not *them*. You know who I mean, our crowd of super-successful, aspirationally desperate

Harvardites. A bunch of nerds who haven't had the nerve to hunt outside the pack before this moment. You know us.

Of course, you don't know us *personally*, but you know what we did last summer, and the summer before that, and the summer before that. You know.

We summered. In the Hamptons. With each other.

When I first took Anna to a dinner party, there was a massive display of wannabe-affection and wannabe-warmth, but all the false façades had passed by the time the main course arrived, when Dome Head started on about her mother.

She gets it all the time; men who want to flex their intellectual muscle with an argument about her mother's theories on nature-versus-nurture. It's a pattern of behaviour I've become familiar with over the time I've spent with Anna. I've also become familiar with the way she reacts. Think missile raids on Kosovo and start multiplying.

Anna speaks her mind for a living. Keeping her cool is anathema to her. That's what I love about her, she doesn't process what she thinks or feels through the filter of etiquette. Maybe my friends are right. Maybe I'll be busted for sharing illicit honesty with her.

I love the way she'll tell a swaying drunk begging for quarters one day to get a life and the next day she'll pass him a ten dollar note and tell him he looks like he needs a drink. The downside of all this honesty is that if she doesn't orgasm, she tells me. Actually, she goes into a snit and orders me back to my own apartment. I doubt she's ever faked anything in her life.

Which brings me back to the lying thing. I've been lying to her, or at least concealing stuff I know she'd want to know. I tell myself it's to protect her, but who am I kidding? Anna doesn't need protection. Truth? I'm scared. Shitting myself scared.

I'm thinking about this problem as I study her, stretched out in the bath, immersed in an inconceivable amount of bubbles.

'Is this razor too blunt do you think?' she asks, wrinkling her nose. There's a tiny bubble on the end of it and I want to kiss it, but I'm worried if I get too close she'll pull me in with her, and I don't really want to dry my suit with her hairdryer again. Last time, it came out all wrinkly like bubble wrap and I had to go into work looking like I'd been thrown in on the wrong cycle.

I hold the disposable blue razor up to the light and assure her it's not too bad.

'You look worried about something,' she states.

I can hardly focus for thinking of all the things I should be saying now. The things I should be revealing. Why am I so weak? If I tell her the truth, maybe she'll just laugh. It's a possibility, but only after she's slashed my carotid artery with the razor, I suspect.

Dragging the razor down her long, lean legs, she looks like an artist at work on a masterpiece. Her Peter Rabbit shower cap like a French beret at a jaunty angle, the Hello Kitty soap dish her pallet.

'Can you hold my toe up closer to my nose,' she asks. 'I need to get a good look at the hairs on my big toe, see?'

I do as instructed.

'And can you light this fag?' she adds, referring to the ever present cigarette lolling sexily from her bee-sting lips.

'You should give up,' I advise her pointlessly.

'I should win a Pulitzer Prize as well, but fate is as fate does.' She shrugs.

I stick a lump of bubbles on her nose. 'It's totally different and you know it. They'll kill you eventually.'

'Yeah right, they can get very bitter those Pulitzer judges, you have to watch your back.'

I light her cigarette and wish I could stop the lying thing.

CHAPTER SEVEN

In this free country I remain enslaved. To fashion. I feel like I'm failing some giant cosmic test every time I catch myself salivating outside a department store window. Part of me would love to be beyond all that and focus on the environment, live in a yurt – wear wooden clogs and clothes made from the skins of beasts, etc. But another part of me would say, 'Who's the designer then?'

I work on it, I really do. As I join the other girls at the sales tables to get the latest in body-disguising, stomach-concealing dresses, I try and think of low environmental impact housing. As I shove another girl aside to get a pair of Jimmy Choos that probably fail every health and safety standard in the world, I try and think of the diminishing world resources. I just don't know that it does much good.

Extract from the 'New York Girl' column of Anna Denier

Anna

Months later and the God-Boy (I must start calling him Mark) is still comfortably ensconced in my flat on Hudson. He stays most nights.

Okay, he stays every night.

Okay, we have favourite sides of the bed.

Okay, we eat together, shower together and sleep together.

And if you really want to split the atom, we have gone over one another's childhood stories with fine-toothed combs.

With everything I learn about him I'm getting in deeper than I ever meant to get. Falling down the rabbit-hole of love. And the further I fall, the harder it's going to be to climb out again.

Since I realised that my feelings for Mark ran deeper than sex, this serialised dream I have, where I'm being locked in my apartment, has started to get totally scary. Now, in the part of the dream when the guys at the party next door are watching me through the two-way mirror, I imagine that I can hear Mark's voice. I am terrified that he is talking to the other guys about me. I can even hear their laughter.

That's when I wake up.

Paranoid? But even paranoids have stuff to be afraid of, right?

The best thing about Mark, apart from the sex, is the way he spoons me at night while we sleep. I have never been spooned before. Normally, I foetal out on one side of the bed, and the guy foetals out on the other. Previously, I thought that spooning was something junkies did to mix up their gear.

I actually love the spooning experience. I have grown used to his body wrapped against mine. I breathe with the regularity of his heartbeat against my back. Sometimes I think my heart is keeping rhythm with his, or maybe we are both just keeping rhythm to the thud of The Prodigy in the apartment opposite.

If I looked deeply into my heart I would have to admit that I am afraid that I couldn't live without this spooning thing if I had to. The thing is, now I feel like a bit of a single-girl fraud. I don't even eat as much cereal as I used to. Sometimes it feels like my relationship with him is a dirty secret I'm dying to confess. My last column briefly touched on letting a guy into the Girl Zone, but I don't think anyone suspected I'd actually tried it myself. Heaven forbid.

By far my greatest concern, though, is the effect that my coupledom might have on my fans. I do have a few, see, and they rely on me to bolster up their faith in singlesville as the most happening spot in which to hang out.

I have a web-site and an e-mail address at the top of my column now so that my hard-core fans can get more of me. More of me than they really need in my opinion. But The Jerk thinks it's important that my readers are able to develop an intimacy with me. He thinks that intimacy is the great catch word of the Millennium. What can I say, he's a very lonely guy. And besides, it's not him who's being cyber-stalked.

Some of the e-mails I get treat me like an agony aunt as opposed to the bewildered cereal-bingeing girl I truly am. I receive several thousand e-mails a week, but I only answer around five a day. Truth is, I don't know what to say to 'Alarmed and Desperate' of New Jersey. I'm sorry that her last boyfriend wanted her to tie him up and urinate on him, but it was my humble opinion that some girls would jump at the chance. So I told her. The Jerk completely lost it.

Mark is very supportive of my job and gives me a shoulder massage when he comes home, which usually turns into an all-over internal massage. It isn't just sex, though. He makes me breakfast every morning and brings it in on a tray with a freshly opened condom which means the breakfast has gone cold by the time I get around to it. He does other stuff too, totally non-sexual stuff. Last week, he bought me an ergonomic keyboard after we broke my other one having sex on it.

Okay, so the other stuff always ends up in sex too, but you see where we're at.

I try and underrate the significance of Mark in my life, even to myself. Although he has hinted repeatedly that he loves me, I have never once hinted it back. I try to laugh when he says it, so as to show him that I don't take it seriously. Or I say existential stuff like, 'What is love . . . really?'

What is my problem? What am I afraid of?

Try: everything.

Fear of fear itself even tempts me to join Sienna who has dropped out altogether. She sent me a postcard from Kathmandu last week where she's been sitting at the feet of a guru for the past month. He's the latest reincarnation of Guru Maj, or someone fat and hirsute like that, and she wants me to join her. TRUTH IS DESTINY she writes at the bottom. And I'm afraid she might be right.

The first few weeks she was gone I just thought she'd had a lot of success with the home-made mustard spell. I guess I was too absorbed with Mark, but now I've really started to miss her and her quirky take on life.

She says that sitting at the feet of this Guru Maj guy takes away all your mental gnawing. I don't think I'm really the type to sit at someone's feet, though. I go into a panic when Mark clips his toenails.

Topsy has been ringing up a lot lately, too. She's dying to meet Mark. They've spoken on the phone a few times. Since that first morning he's been reluctant to mention her, but I can tell he still idolises her. She's coming to The Pierre this weekend for a few weeks and he can't hide his excitement. My mother doesn't visit cities, see, she visits hotels. The Peninsular in LA, The George V in Paris, Claridges in London.

I'll Have Mine On The Rocks! is still on the bestseller list. And I would have to be totally dense not to notice that I am *persona non grata* in large sections of American society. I have even received hate mail from people who assume that I came via an ice-dispensing machine.

Mark's on the phone to Topsy now as I proofread my latest column before sending it off. I hear him laughing at something she's said and feel troubled. They are finalising the brunch on Sunday at Nadine's. Nadine's has become Mark's and my home away from home, and a part of me doesn't want to share this love-spot with my mother.

He would have met her sooner but she has been touring the country doing book signings and having eggs thrown at her. Not everyone is lapping up her theories on women putting their eggs on ice for the future. In fact, a lot of people think a woman's eggs should come straight up. How God intended.

There is a movement gathering momentum in parts of Middle America that wants to stage a mass burning of my mother's book. Unlike Mark, I have yet to read it. For a million and one depressing reasons I have sworn off reading my mother's books.

He replaces the handset in the cradle and comes over to me. 'She's so cool your mom. I'm can't wait to actually meet her in person.'

He has no idea how this remark hurts me.

The fact that my mother already has a pet name for him – Cupcake – troubles me as well. She has forgotten, but I haven't, that this was also her pet name for my dad. Or maybe she hasn't forgotten. Maybe it is all a set-up. Maybe Topsy planned for Mark and me to get together years ago. Maybe she had him put on ice for me.

I fear for myself sometimes. I worry about falling in love with a guy who isn't real. I worry about being let down and about having my heart broken. And that is why I try and stay objective. I can't allow myself to trust Mark. I tell myself that the reason he's staying with me is merely a pragmatic convenience. He has his sister staying in his apartment, see. That's the only reason he stays over so much, surely?

'Alex is making a point,' Mark explains to me when I ask him why his sister's been staying so long. She moved in while getting her shit together after a big argument with her husband, who, it transpires, wants a son very much. Foreskin and all.

Part of the way his sister is getting her shit together, apparently, is by kick-boxing a life size effigy of her husband, Marty. My mother expounded this kind of thing on the Oprah Winfrey show years ago. I can see how Mark might find watching his sister relentlessly pounding the effigy with her feet disconcerting. In that sense anyway, my flat and the spooning of my body night after night is probably preferable.

That's what I try and tell myself.

I can't allow myself to relax in this relationship. The safe, lonely future of cereal-eating spinsterhood isn't so clear now. I can't allow myself to think of what the future holds anymore, just in case it isn't Mark. The Upper East Side girl inside me has no such qualms. Mentally, she is already redecorating Mark's large, air-conditioned Upper East Side apartment and packing his sister back to Marty.

The words 'large' and 'air-conditioned' speak volumes to me especially when the temperature rises above one hundred degrees. I say that Mark is 'comfortably' ensconced with me but it is a little cramped, actually. August is even hotter than July. July was very bad indeed.

At one point on the subway I thought I was going to expire. I even fainted, but a man with a large bruise on his forehead brought me round by riffling round in my Wonderbra. He said he was only trying to rob me. I must be a real new Yorker because I believed he was telling the truth.

Later on in the evening, as a hot breeze comes through the window, I think of what it must be like to have air-conditioning. 'Tell me about your apartment on the Upper East Side again?' I plead, the way dying soldiers of war plead with their comrades to tell them once more about Kentucky.

'You'd hate it. It is totally not you,' he tells me, moving in for a snog. 'It's not even me. I haven't gotten round to decorating even. I bought it because it's near work, but I'd much rather live around here.'

I can't reply because the kissing begins. He is a serious kisser and it takes all my concentration. Sometimes we kiss for hours. Sometimes he kisses me awake. I have to apply a moisturising lip-balm constantly.

'The air-conditioning sounds kinda cool,' I suggest hopefully, coming up for breath.

But he doesn't appear to have heard me. 'Hey, listen to this, I read it earlier,' he digresses. Reaching over for the paper he reads out another feature article on my mother. When he's done, he says, 'What a load of crow. Do you think the bitch even read the book?'

I blush, but say nothing. This bitch in his arms hasn't read the book herself so I'm not going to be the one to cast the first stone. I blow on my chest some more and try to look as hot as I can without being totally unappealing.

'What's up?' he asks.

'Oh, nothing,' I sigh, blowing harder. 'It's just so hot in this little apartment,' I murmur, snuggling into his body. He puts his arms around me then and I melt – in every sense of the word. 'Do you think your sister will ever move out? Is there really no way we could spend some time in your apartment?' I whisper, swooning in the sweet male smell of his shirt.

'Hon, I can't kick my own sister out. Where would she go?'

'How about here?' I propose, without giving the matter any thought.

'Here?'

'Yeah, on Hudson? It's a very hip place to live, actually.'

He laughs and ruffles my hair which badly needs a wash.

'What's the matter with Hudson?' I ask, feeling v. patronised.

'Nothing's the matter with Hudson. I love Hudson, I love this hood, I love you.' He pulls me in for a kiss and I can tell it's a lost cause. What was I thinking? His sister would never fit her life-sized effigy of Marty into my apartment.

Besides, Mark has given up plenty of things for me. His parents, for instance. They have a place in the Hamptons but Mark has avoided the privilege of spending time there to be with me. He says it's because he's sick of the place. I think it's because I'm not invited. And I suspect the reason I'm not invited is because of my mother's book.

CHAPTER EIGHT

Mothers are embarrassing. All mothers. And it doesn't get easier as you age. If anything, your resistance just gets lower.

I have this dream of my mother jauntily pushing me down Fifth Ave. in a wheelchair when I'm eighty. She'll still be this amazing, gorgeous, sprightly young thing, while I'm a shrivelled old woman with grey hair and bandaged legs.

I may not be shrivelled and bandaged quite yet, but I feel that way whenever I'm with my mother.

Extract from the 'New York Girl' column of Anna Denier

Anna

When the day of Brunch With Topsy arrives, I am feeling like hell with some gastric thing, probably to do with eating oysters in a month without an R. I'd become a bit of an oyster junkie since Mark.

Because I am feeling so crap, I don't spend enough time on my wardrobe or makeup. Mark changes the subject when I ask him how I look which is always a bad sign.

I expect to be upstaged by Topsy anyway. As she never tires of reminding me, she is the woman who put the sex into the sex wars. The diva to bust all divas. As it is, I make the busboys look serene, and in New York this is ultimate power failure. Mark squeezes my hand supportively as I introduce him to Topsy.

The sun is blazing on the queue outside Nadine's when we arrive, exposing the flaws on everyone but my mother. Topsy's presence ensures that we are led straight to our centre stage table. Sitting amongst the decadent downtown chic of Nadine's, she looks resplendent – the queen bee incarnate. Mark buzzes about her happily while I watch on miserably, very much the drone.

She is wearing a tight black wool jersey dress that emphasises the Denier skeletal frame, her untouched red hair pulled back in a perfect chignon. I have to give it to her, she looks unutterably glamorous. People don't look like my mother anymore, not in cities like New York and London anyway. The pace and the attitude takes it out of you. I ask you, who can maintain glamour in a New York cab, let alone the subway?

'Isn't this rustic darlings?' Topsy trills. Any place without marble floors and loads of gold gilt is rustic to Topsy. Mark and I are seated opposite her, holding hands like teenagers, and I like to think that we look like a pretty cute couple. Mark at least makes up one half of a cute couple, maybe I just look like a girl who got lucky.

I always obsess about my appearance in the company of my mother. My neuroses start to nag, convincing me that the people looking on are thinking I must be either incredibly powerful or rich or both to land a God-Boy.

Topsy doesn't take long to pick up on my insecurities. Why would she? She installed the chip in the first place.

'You look like you've just been rescued from a soup kitchen in Alphabet City,' she announces loudly, smoothing a heavily bejewelled hand over her sleek hair.

'She's been throwing up,' Mark explains, reddening. 'All morning. For the last few days, haven't you, Anna?'

In the ensuing silence I just sit there and bite my lip. My father used to call it waiting for shit to fall. So you can see where I get my great way with words.

And I know it's going to be bad when Topsy arches one perfectly drawn eyebrow and says pointedly, 'Throwing up? Throwing up in the morning? Eggnog?'

'What?' I mutter, knowing that the shit has started falling but totally clueless vis-à-vis mounting a defence, despite my years of experience with Topsy and her propensity for high drama.

'Well, it's obvious isn't it?' Topsy sighs.

'Huh?'

'Do I have to spell it out?'

Mark starts nodding furiously.

'Morning sickness.'

I roll my eyes. It wasn't as bad as I thought. I thought she was going to start on about bulimia and my insecurities and refer to a bad patch I had when I was fourteen. She caught me shovelling a packet of white bread down my neck at midnight and spent the rest of my adolescence churning out the story for audiences across America. My Struggle With A Teenage Bulimic. The nation's heart went out to her – really.

No, this wasn't as bad as that. This was Topsy in low gear; even feeling nauseous I could handle this. I shake my head and smile at her and Mark. 'Food poisoning,' I say firmly. 'Bad oyster. What are you having Mark?'

Topsy sighs again, with a greater sense of pathos this time, and something deep within my subconscious squirms. 'I thought you'd learnt enough about safe sex by now, Eggnog!' She makes this pronouncement in a really loud voice. I don't look around but I can tell people are staring. They probably think my mother is a Good Samaritan and I am her latest good cause, a hooker she's helping off the streets.

'Of course I practise safe sex!' I scream back. I feel Mark's hand cringe in mine. The crowded restaurant collectively lose all interest in their pancakes and mimosas and turn their full attention to us. 'Of course I bloody do. Tell her Mark!' I nudge him hard in the ribs.

He quietly assures Topsy that condoms are a number one priority with both of us. But that subconscious squirming thing has got the better of me.

'Tell her about the knots Mark, tell her how you tie the knots. He's so into safe sex he ties knots!' I hiss. 'Tell her Mark!'

He grips my hand so hard I feel the circulation stop.

Our table lapses into silence for a while as the wannabe-actress waitress I silently name My Pal (owing to the understanding wink she gives me as my mother cries out for Bollinger in a voice that could break glass) passes out the menus. This is my childhood revisited. No public outing was complete without a scene. Every move my mother made was a curtain call for the rest of us. I look at Mark shrinking into his T-shirt like a turtle. I'm reasonably sure that Topsy isn't quite what he was expecting. He thought he was getting Joan Rivers, now here he is with Joanna Lumley's Patsy – on uberoverdrive.

I try and take his hand again for a reassuring squeeze but it's disappeared somewhere under the table. This is when I first begin to panic that he might be taking the stuff my mother said with more than the grain of salt it deserves.

Surrounding diners are just about to go back to their own conversations when my mother announces in her tannoy voice that I look puffy. The champagne is being poured as I reply calmly, 'That's because it is over ninety degrees.'

'I was puffy with her,' she tells My Pal. 'You should have seen what she did to my stomach. The scarring was horrific. My lesbian midwife said she'd never seen anything like it.' My Pal smiles supportively in my direction as she puts the bottle in the bucket.

'Drop it will you, Topsy. I told you I've had food poisoning.' My Pal shakes her head in sympathy as she leaves. Watching her go, I feel abandoned.

Topsy raises her eyes to heaven as if I have said something obscene. She turns to Mark. 'I just want you to know, Cupcake, she didn't get this uptight attitude from me.'

I glare at her in warning.

She ignores me. 'Like her attitude on cleanliness, it comes from her father's genetic pool, which is more of a pond really.'

My mother told me when I was going to live with Dad that there were two things I needed to know about him. One was that he never changed his underwear, and the other was that his genetic readout read 'asshole'. So I know that being compared to my dad is not a good thing.

I think Mark does too. He asks politely about the weather in San Francisco in a brave attempt to steer the conversation onto safer ground. Having heard my stories about my father and Topsy and their dynamics, he knows it's a minefield he doesn't want to traverse.

I try and study the menu but I don't feel like eating. Even though I feel a bit iffy belly wise, I long for hard liquor and I don't think the champagne will be enough. I suspect this situation may call for vodka. I look at Topsy as her laughter tinkles through the restaurant and I clock the looks of awe being cast at our table by other diners. My mother, the icon.

Her earlier remark about my sense of cleanliness coming from my father has cut especially deep. I know there is a certain hygiene menace lurking in my kitchen but the rest of my apartment is pretty neat. A bit chaotic perhaps, but coy. I do actually use a bleach on my bathroom weekly, despite the cost to the environment as outlined by Sienna, who uses tea tree oil to clean everything from her clothes to the toilet, which I find so gross I can't speak to her about it. Thinking about Sienna cheers me up, though. I have started to miss her quite a lot.

I catch snatches of Mark and Topsy's conversation as I dwell on the injustice of it all. Stories of my father's failed attempts to produce films. Stories of my mother's huge success as an author. Stories of my own failure to form lasting relationships with men.

'Will you shut up? Mark doesn't want to know all

that,' I interrupt, sounding discordant and irrational like those lunatics on the B-train. My mother always brings out the worst in me.

Watching Mark as he attempts to disappear inside the overly large menu, I try and get a grip. This is the first time he has seen us together and I know who is coming off looking best.

My stomach starts to rumble and Topsy looks at me with an extravagant show of knowing sympathy. 'Poor Eggnog,' she sighs.

'What?' I ask.

She smiles sweetly, plants a kiss on her finger and blows it across to me. 'Pregnancy is nature's cruellest joke, Eggnog.'

My jaw falls into my lap. 'Oh fuck, shit, bugger, bum, why are you doing this?'

Topsy looks shocked by my language. 'Is this the sort of hip-chick talk you picked up in London? Or are you going to blame this on the morning sickness as well?' she asks, rolling her eyes at Mark.

'Morning sickness?' he exclaims, looking v. seriously worried now.

'Will you cut the morning sickness gag?' I snap, astonished at her ability to push my buttons. 'Ignore her Mark, it's just one of Topsy's private parlour games.' I turn to Topsy. 'And I don't want to play. You're drunk on your own hype!' The words are out of my mouth before I realise how loudly I am shouting and how mean I must sound.

Topsy turns her attention to Mark again as if I haven't said a word. 'You wouldn't believe the morning sickness I got with this one.' She points at me with one long blood-red nail as if I am one of a large litter of ratlings rather than her human offspring.

Trying to appear neutral, he nods in his non-committal legal way and squeezes my hand again under the table. He's being a complete darling and I try and pull the brunch together for his sake.

'Isn't he lovely?' she asks. I'm about to answer in the affirmative when she adds, 'Compared to your usual boyfriend material, he's a veritable . . . what's the term?'

'God-Boy?' I mutter.

Even when we agree on something, Topsy manages to wind me up. I feel my blood pressure rising as she goes on to amuse Mark with tales of the men I've previously dated. I start to gnaw on my nails like a savage. It is all I can do to stop myself muttering foul curses under my breath like the woman who pushes the shopping trolleys piled with trash down our street. Sienna has this book on voodoo and I wish now that I'd read it more carefully when I leafed through it one time. At the time I'd thought it *très* weird, but now I need something or someone I can stick pins into. Badly.

'Oh, and then there was that artist with the goatee!' she squawks, as I tug at a particularly tough cuticle with my teeth and draw blood.

Mark laughs as Topsy goes on to outline all the odious features of the guy in question. This is all I need. Mark and I haven't actually got round to describing one another's past lovers in any detail yet. We'd held up our score cards, natch, but I'd covered my spate of dating goatee-chinned artists from Shoreditch in one broad stroke as my 'bohemian stage'. I didn't want Mark thinking he was my lucky break.

He whispers in my ear, 'If you're feeling like you're not up for this Anna, if you want to escape, I can take you back home.' He turns to Topsy. 'I don't think Anna's feeling too well,' he says, as he rubs my lower back. I smile weakly and shrug at my mother.

'She'll have to get used to the nausea, Mark,' she warns him solemnly. 'Morning sickness can last the whole first trimester, and beyond if you're unlucky. And when that's over you just get fatter and fatter and fatter until someone pulls the little alien—'

'Enough!' I snap. 'It's not funny you know. We told you that we use condoms. I am not pregnant. This is not morning sickness. I ate a bad oyster, end of story.' I hold the menu up to signify that we've finished with the issue.

'I'll have the organic muffin with orange butter,' Mark says as My Pal arrives to take our order.

'I'll have the vodka,' I say.

'News flash, youngsters! Condoms can burst,' Topsy announces *sotto voce*.

'What are you talking about?' I shriek.

'What brand do you use? Aladdin? If you don't use the reinforced balloon thickness ones, you can bet your life they'll leak.'

Mark squeaks, 'Actually the vodka sounds really refreshing. Let's have a bottle,' he suggests.

'Well Eggnog shouldn't be drinking spirits when she's pregnant. You don't want a defective kid do you, Mark?' she asks. My Pal touches me on the shoulder.

'Why are you doing this?' I hiss over the top of the menu.

Topsy merely shrugs and gives me a weary I-try-my-best look. 'I think you're being naive, that's all,' she says with real concern in her voice. 'Most condom brands have an astonishingly high failure rate, isn't that true?' she asks, turning to My Pal.

My Pal goes as red as Topsy's hair. 'I s'pose,' she says, wishing she'd landed that job on the chorus of *Les Mis* – any job other than this one.

'Of course, you'll have to say good-bye to your waistline forever, Eggnog.'

I make a squeaking sound.

'Well, it's better she faces it now, Mark. She'll have to say good-bye to her figure.' Her lower lip drops as if my loss of figure will break her heart.

Mark ignores the remark but I notice tiny beads of perspiration gathering on his brow. Caught between the cross-fire of his idol and his lover, who can blame him for feeling rattled? I only hope he isn't taking Topsy and her talk of pregnancy seriously.

My Pal takes the opportunity to high-tail it. I want to run after her and see if they need any help in the kitchen.

'Honestly, you should read the reports. Every second condom is a dud these days.'

'Bit like mothers,' I snap, regretting the words as they fly out of my mouth. Not because she is anything other than a lunatic mother, but because I'd come out without my stun gun.

I notice Mark out of the corner of my eye, rearranging his cutlery nervously like a small country manoeuvring a case for neutrality at the UN.

'Oh, is this what your pregnancy is all about, Eggnog?' she asks. 'This is your way of saying I wasn't a good mother. Is that it?'

'Okay, enough. Either you shut up about pregnancy or I leave. Period!'

'Or lack thereof,' Topsy mutters in a stage whisper. If I wasn't trying to avoid high-karma situations I would wrap my fallopian tubes around her neck and strangle her.

'If you're not sure whether you're pregnant or not, have a test,' she advises in a really calm voice I wasn't familiar with. 'But for goodness sake don't dump your insecurities on me. I have the most exhausting schedule.'

'What's my pregnancy got to do with your schedule?' I demand, before I realise that I'm giving credence to her madness.

'Do you think you might be pregnant then?' Mark gasps, suddenly rejoining the conversation.

Topsy starts throwing her arms out like a Shakespearean heroine. 'I have no vocation for grannydom.'

'Will you just shut up and drink your fucking champagne!' I shout.

She looks at me in horror as if I've told her I'm about to shoot her. 'Why are you doing this to me, Eggnog? Why?' My lower jaw is still clattering about on the floor like a dropped plate when she changes tack and smiles. 'I'll help to coach you for the birth, Eggnog. You know I wouldn't let you down on that side.' She starts pulling out her diary and flicking through the pages. 'Only I'll need a firm date. When are you due?'

I feel like a victim of some cosmic joke. I could see the headlines, 'I'll Have Mine On The Rocks Daughter In Love Child Scandal'.

There is a one in a million chance that I could be pregnant. I mean, we really had always practised safe sex. There had been one accident but I am almost positive that it occurred in my last cycle. But not that positive. Then there is the late thing – as in I *am* late. But then I'm always running late. Running over deadlines like truckers run down critters on the road. And my cycle is no different.

Put it this way, the possibility that I could be pregnant is slim enough to get down the cat-walk, but it is there. Smug, whiny, irritating, but there, sending me running to the loo where I throw up again.

After brunch with my mother Mark confronts me with the question. 'Is it possible that you *are* pregnant?'

And even though I tell him I'm not, somehow I let it slip that I am two weeks late. That is enough. Without further discussion, he has his sister move out of his apartment and we move in. Without even meaning to I have become one of those ruthless Manhattan bitches who will do anything to score an air-conditioned apartment on the Upper East Side.

CHAPTER NINE

The number of breeders per capita in New York has escalated and something must be done. Single girls desperately need a sharp influx of single men if casual sex in New York is to continue.

Pregnancy power and the joy of coupledom aside, couples and their offspring take up space that single guys could use.

From the web-site of Anna Denier:
http//www.Annadishes.com

Mark

Rob is on the other end of the line, telling me how much he wants me to be his best man. He doesn't have to lay it on this thick, of course I'd be happy to. I drift off and think of other things but moments later I hear Rob shouting down the phone line, breaking my reverie. 'It sounds great Rob,' I promise, pulling my brain into gear.

'You don't have to sound so keen,' he mutters sarcastically.

But I am keen. Honestly. Last year I'd have been dancing on my desk at the invitation. It is the perfect role for me. I was born to be the other guy's best man. In fact, I'd been best man so many times I could do it professionally, hire myself out. I have the outfit, I'm ready to go at a moment's notice. I'm not boasting when I say I'm highly valued on the wedding circuit of my friends; loved by guys and trusted by their fiancées. And that is no easy feat.

A best man has to be a good friend, organised and calm at all times, even when he's raising the roof or smashed out of his skull. The best man has to keep it together. All things to all men. Ready to throw a stag night one night and sober up a nervous groom the next morning. Without wanting to brag, there is a lot of skill involved, and happily for my friends and family, I'm the master.

Face it, it's a job custom-made for jerks who don't want to commit themselves.

I start telling Rob why I was distracted. 'This big case I told you about wants to settle. I guess I was distracted for a minute there, but seriously, you know I'd be honoured to be your best man, Rob. Why don't we meet up for a drink after work to celebrate?' I suggest.

PS: What I'm really saying here is, why don't you give me the perfect excuse not to go home tonight?

I need an out, bad.

Mollified, Rob agrees to meet and starts telling me about Rebecca's plans for the stag night she wants me to throw. Something about separate rooms in a hotel. Then he reminds me about his dinner party tomorrow night, which is fortuitous because I had actually forgotten. Since Anna's pregnancy my brain feels like it's got a virus.

Larna, my secretary, finally wanders in with my coffee. She's five months pregnant herself and the bulge under her dress terrifies me. We kissed five years ago at the firm's Christmas party. That's all – just kissed. But every time I see her bulge now I think of that kiss. It wasn't even a good kiss or a mutually sought kiss. She sort of lunged and I sort of obliged, kissing her out of politeness more than anything else.

I'll have one of those bulges soon, or rather Anna will. I motion to Larna to put the coffee on my desk and leave. After I've wrapped up the call with Rob, I take a sip of the coffee and scald my mouth. Suddenly, holding myself together and just getting on with it is no longer a viable option. Anna's picture is on my desk. She's grinning, adorable. Kissable.

Pregnant!

I need air. I need to get out and clear my head. I tell Larna that I've got to pick something up for Anna and ask her to field my calls. 'I won't be long,' I promise, knowing that I will but I am so good at lying now, she doesn't suspect a thing.

'Sure,' she smiles breezily and goes back to her work.

Amazing. She trusts me. I wish she wouldn't. And it's not just her. Everyone trusts me and they really, really shouldn't. Other people's trust is about the biggest burden a guy can have thrust on him. I'm not ready for trust. I'm not ready for fatherhood, for a mapped-out future.

Saks is crowded but I stride purposefully through the lunchtime workers as I make my way towards the elevator. I'm a man on a mission and my fellow shoppers know it. They recognise the gait of a serious buyer as opposed to a lunchtime or out of town browser. My mission is one of deceit and denial but that doesn't make it unworthy. Deceit and denial are all part of a deeper love.

When the girl and you fall in love and she tells you she might be pregnant, you rejoice. Now that's not negotiable, that's a fact. It's a rule. It doesn't matter that you both agreed you didn't want kids, it doesn't matter that you've always been careful, used condoms every time, tied the knot and believed yourself safe from disaster. None of that matters.

Being thrilled about your girlfriend's pregnancy is like the most ancient ritual, worked out in the caves during the dawn of time when the only power a woman had was the power to carry human life. Topsy goes on about it all the time. Because it was once the only power in a woman's hands, it remains the ultimate Woman Tool.

Let's just say, when Anna told me there was a chance she could be pregnant, I went into caveman overdrive.

'Wow!' I exclaimed in a whizzed up hyper-excited voice I hadn't heard myself use since my eighth birthday when I was presented with my first set of blades. 'That's so . . .'

'So?'

'Wow!'

Anna was as calm as I was excited. It was as if she got pregnant every day of the week. 'Don't get too excited. It's very unlikely. I'm only a few weeks late remember. And it's not official,' she added hastily, as if to stem my joy which was bursting out of me.

'A few weeks! That's huge. That is definitely official,' I assured her. 'But how did it happen?' This question was much more important to me than I made out at the time.

She shrugged. 'Dunno, it must have been a miracle.'

'It must have,' I agreed with more fervour than I let show.

And that is the thing. Given that it's a miracle, a huge, huge feat of accomplishment and wonder, I kind of think it is churlish not to be thrilled. No arguments. Fine. I'm thrilled, grateful, down on my knees. Totally awed and over the fucking moon.

Face it, who am I fooling? I'm gutted, as Anna would put it. It's how I imagine being on the luge must feel.

Once I'd taken her in my arms and said 'Wow!', it was as if fate had strapped me on and sent me off, hurtling down the slopes to my inevitably disastrous conclusion.

Anna kept saying that it was highly unlikely that she was anything other than overdue. She said that even if she was pregnant, it was the last thing she wanted. But I wasn't going to fall into that old trap. That day could be one of those moments in my life that I'd be looking back on forever – the day I was told I was going to be a father.

'Is that cash or card?' the guy asks.

'Cash,' I reply, feeling like a criminal as I hand over the notes.

CHAPTER TEN

We can't keep kidding ourselves — most women only use their wombs as a last resort because, well . . . they are pushed for time, basically.

As a concept, biological clocks didn't even exist a hundred years ago. Back then, women started pumping out kids from the day they started having sex. Maybe it's all a myth, maybe our time will never run out. To this end, scientists everywhere are working on an elixir — or some sort of cloning alternative! And I for one wish them every success. In a few years' time, with a bit of luck, thirty-somethings might be ordering embalming fluid shots at trendy late-night bars while sheep give birth for them.

Extract from *I'll Have Mine On The Rocks!* by Topsy Denier

Anna

Despite the fact that I have mentioned my lack of interest in *ever* reproducing the Denier line, Mark's own excitement at the prospect of fatherhood has obviously overwritten all details. I haven't even dared suggest other options in the event that I *am* pregnant. The shock could kill him. But he must have noticed that I'm not thrilled – unless he secretly buys into the all-girls-are-born-mothers propaganda that Topsy is always going on about.

Sienna had arrived back from Kathmandu with a slipper from the foot of Guru Maj to worship, and when I go downtown to my apartment to collect a few things, she invites me down to her space (her word) for a chi (a sort of sickly sweet tea-like drink made from cardamom and Yak fat that tastes like sweat).

When I tell her about my fear that I might be pregnant, she kindly offers to lend me the slipper, 'To call down my true destiny,' as she puts it. She hands said footwear over and I try not to gag too obviously.

I don't need to check it with forensics to recognise that Guru Maj has been wearing the slipper pretty recently. It stinks.

PS: The guy is a spiritual leader to thousands and he can't get an odour-eater together? Hello?

I hold it away from my body gingerly. It is an enormous, saggy, leather thing, held together with dubious stitching. The front is pointed like a pixie shoe but, owing to wear, it has split open into a sort of macabre grin. What was once colourful embroidery is now grimy with dirt and sweat. It is so hideous I find it difficult to believe that even Sienna would have anything to do with it. New-age and all, the slipper is too gross.

As evidence of how desperate I am, though, I accept her offer gratefully and race home with it to draw down my true destiny which, let's face it, has to be better than the poxy destiny I am presently stuck with.

Back in Mark's apartment, I place it on the glass dining table and wonder if I am really losing the plot or whether I just never had a strong grip on it in the first place. The slipper looks even more out of place in Mark's tribute to clinical minimalism than me and my toys. I am sitting on the floor looking up at it and a cheaper more styleless piece of footwear I can't imagine. But hey, if it is going to bring me inner peace and true desire, I am all for it.

'What do I do?' I'd asked Sienna when she sent me home, armed with the smelly grail. I imagined there might be a chant or an affirmation involved.

'Nothing,' Sienna said.

'Nothing?'

'Just *be* the slipper.'

'*Be* the slipper?'

'*Be* the slipper,' she confirmed. She'd become a girl of few words since Kathmandu. The word 'be' featured heavily, though.

Looking at the sweaty article of leather now, I start to have second thoughts and give her a ring. 'Does it have to be *this* slipper in particular? I mean, are you sure a vintage Jimmy Choo wouldn't do just as well? A shoe's a shoe after all. Aren't they all just symbols of—'

She is resolute. 'Respect, Anna, respect. Guru Maj has worn that slipper for years. It's a sacred slipper.'

'Same could be said for Jimmy,' I mutter, but she chooses not to hear.

'Trust me on this, Anna. If you can't take my advice on matters of the esoteric, whose can you take? The slipper will bring you the fulfilment and destiny you crave if it's true. *Be* the slipper. Worship.'

So worship the slipper I do. To the best of my ability. I focus on destiny and truth and how much I don't want to be with child. I do this for, oh, I don't know, well over an hour I think. And before you laugh, let me tell you, it actually works. Yes, it works!

I notice the blood on my knickers at lunchtime.

You'd think I'd be rejoicing, wouldn't you? One minute terrified by the prospect of motherhood, the next minute the scare completely over. A false alarm. Phew!

You'd think I'd wrap my arms around that smelly slipper and chant Guru Maj's name from every rooftop in Manhattan. But instead I feel sick with shame. Guilty for getting Mark so excited and having to let him down. How am I ever going to break the news of Guru Maj's miracle to Mark?

It's not as if I'd bought into the pregnancy myth, but Mark had. And bought in a lot more heavily than I could ever have imagined. I mean, we'd talked about how much neither of us wanted kids but he'd done a rapid about face when he heard he was going to be a dad. He'd bought every excitement share on the father-to-be market and I know his heart will be broken.

I dither for hours around the phone. Picking up the handpiece and putting it down again. Even when he calls me to tell me that he'll be coming home late the words get stuck in my throat.

I mope around the large Upper East Side apartment with views of Central Park – the apartment from which we have ejected his sister. I feel bloated and miserable, like Mr Snufflupugus, (only not quite that big, obviously). I feel ridiculously out of place, though. I find the features of the place – AC, view of the park, costumed doorman, proximity to tourists and smart shops with polished brass fixtures – oppressive.

I try to admire the view. Sienna said she was really envious; she said that I should picture it as a big green lung, but that just grosses me out. I would rather be looking out on the view from my Hudson Street flat – the view that's not really a view at all, more a block of dingy one-bedroom apartments like my own, actually. Oh, how I long for the aggressive sounds of Prodigy again. 'Smack My Bitch Up' seems like a sweet symphony from a golden age of bohemian fabness compared to the clinical splendour of Central Park. Besides, all this green can't be good for me. It's never been my colour. And where is the creative inspiration in a view that people recognise from postcards?

Mark's sister Alex rings to congratulate me in the afternoon. She's moved back in with her husband and patched things up. 'What's in a foreskin after all?' she decrees. I should have said something other than 'blood' but I am feeling in v. bad spirits.

It isn't just Mark I'm going to have to hurt. His whole family and most of his friends are in on it now. All I'd done was miss a period and suddenly I am flavour of the month, although I know my popularity shares are going to plummet in value once the truth is out.

I am in a very high-karma situation.

I look pleadingly at the slipper of Guru Maj propped on the glass dining table, hoping it might have another miracle lurking in the inner sole, but it would probably take more than a worn-out size thirteen slipper to take away this guilt I am feeling. Unless two is better than one that is. Maybe what one slipper can't manage, two can? Hopelessly hopeful, I ring Sienna and ask where the other slipper in the pair is.

'Oh, he only had the one,' she explains breezily. I envisage her swanning around in her caftan, lighting incense in the cardinal points of her dark little apartment. She is remarkably calm and serene, an all-round advertisement for new-age awareness. But what I hear next totally grosses me out. 'His mother chopped his other foot off when he was a little boy in Varanessi.'

New-agers can be so callous. Oh, they go on and on

about the rights of a mink and the evils of capitalism, but give them a human body part and they're as casual as can be. Well, I'm not going to stand for it. 'What a bitch,' I squawk, appalled that a mother could do such a thing to her own kid. No wonder he'd got so fervently behind my prayer to be infertile. His own experiences as a child would put even the most hopeful Guru off reproduction.

'He had gangrene,' she explains reasonably. 'Something about an accident and a train. It was amputation or death.'

I mumble something about that being another matter.

'Not that it held Guru Maj back. He's walked all over the Himalayas and India.'

'Which would actually be hopping,' I point out, being the pragmatist, in this friendship at least.

'Whatever. You can keep the slipper for longer if you want, see what happens. It may well give you the strength you need to reveal your falsehood. Truth is destiny, after all.'

I thank her, but the thought of gangrene – even if it is in the other foot – puts me off the slipper. It is all so bloody unfair. This pregnancy scare is a v. bad omen and Topsy the harbinger. It is all her fault, Topsy and her damnable obsession with reproduction.

CHAPTER ELEVEN

Lies. It's all lies.

Girls lie. No matter what we tell boys, we can't lie to ourselves. Honestly. We lie.

We start off in the playground, telling our friends that they look great, when they don't.

We tell the teacher we did our reading, when we didn't.

Tell our parents we are still virgins, when we're not.

Tell guys it's big, when it's far from it.

Tell guys we've come, when we weren't even close.

Imagine what would happen if we stopped telling lies? If girls stopped lying, the world would stop turning.

Extract from the 'New York Girl' column of Anna Denier

Anna

'Men have used women's menstruation to subjugate women over the centuries,' Topsy chants happily when I call her and tell her that *everything* is her fault.

'It's nothing to do with women's menstruation. None of this would have bloody happened if it wasn't for you. It's all your fault,' I insist. 'Everything! If you hadn't got him started on the idea, I wouldn't be in this mess.'

'Eggnog, can't you see? You're falling into the trap of transferring your guilt onto me. This is what men want women to do. Turning us against each other is how they steal our wind.'

'What's wind got to do with anything?' I ask, as I paint my nails a new henna colour that Sienna brought back with her from Nepal.

Topsy rants on about the oppressive nature of men, but I've heard it all before. Sometimes just the word oppression makes me gag. 'I can't believe you don't realise how they use our cycles to turn us against each other. It suits them that we blame one another. Just like the way you are blaming me now.'

'It's nothing to do with wind or cycles or oppression. He's thrown his sister out of his flat for me. He's told his parents that I'm carrying their grandchild. He's asked me to marry him.'

She whoops for joy. 'Oh goody, a celebration, I'll bring round champagne.'

'You'll do no such thing,' I tell her firmly.

'Did he give you a ring?' Always the romantic, my mother.

'Yes,' I admit. 'He gave me a ring. I didn't accept it, naturally.'

'Whyever not?' My not accepting Mark's ring is the first thing to really bring emotion to Topsy's voice. She simply adores jewellery.

'I didn't accept it because I'm not marrying a man just because I'm pregnant.'

'Well there you are, problem solved. You're not pregnant, there's nothing to stand in your way. Oh darling, Topsy loves a wedding,' she squeals. 'I know this divine lesbian celebrant who can marry you. Her name's Liz Nipple.'

'Oh shut up,' I groan.

'Don't you think that's a fabulous name? It's a pity you're not pregnant, really. Nipples Denier? It works, doesn't it?'

'It so does *not* work,' I inform her. 'Are you eating those mushrooms again or something, Topsy? You know they've proved a link between them and loss of orgasm ability?'

She ignores me. 'Topsy loves a wedding. Despite being a patriarchal form of men laying claim to women, everyone looks so divine. All that pageantry and ritual. I sometimes think I ought to have been a druid.'

I look at Madeleine slumped in the corner, disgustingly disillusioned for a little French orphaned school girl. I want to cry. I wish Topsy could have been a druid, too. If she had been a druid she wouldn't have been able to screw up my life. She would have been too busy gallivanting around Stonehenge and baking ley-line cookies to give birth to me. I could have been born the child of a nice normal couple, a woman who let me call her Mom and told my father to plump the scatter cushions. So unfair.

Vainly, I try to explain the predicament she's put me in. 'The point is, Topsy, the reason Mark wants to marry me is because he thinks that I am carrying his child. He actually wants a baby, see. He didn't before the scare but now it seems he actually *aspires* to fatherhood and all the perks, one of which is kids. Don't you see what that signifies?'

My voice has hit a high note but Topsy's sounds

like pure syrup. 'Of course I do. What a lucky little Eggnog you are. Think of all those single mothers out there who have to get by without support from society or family, let alone a lovely boy like Mark.'

I try to bring things back on track. 'You keep refusing to face the fact that I'm not even pregnant though, Topsy. Not only that, but I never want to have children. Like . . . let me see? Ever!'

'Not ever?'

'Well, not in the foreseeable future.'

'So what are you complaining about? You've got a lovely man, a lovely apartment, the offer of a lovely ring and no reason for irregular weight gain?'

'God I hate you.'

'No, no, no, no. It's not me you hate, Eggnog. You're the victim of men, and not just in this lifetime but in all your past lives, too. This has been going on since time began.'

Okay, so now I am certain. She's definitely been taking something.

'I still hate you,' I sulk. I hear a hiccup on the other end of the line. As I suspected, it isn't Topsy talking, it is the champagne.

'By the way, Eggnog, Oprah Winfrey wants you to appear with me to discuss your decision to become pregnant. It seems that the American people want to know why you didn't take my advice to young women everywhere on freezing your eggs for the future.'

'You are so, so sick – you do see that, don't you?'

'What? It would be great publicity.'

I throw the phone across the vast, white carpeted floor and swear in languages I never knew I had a grasp of. Then I sob. Big, hard, ugly sounds come out of me as I cast all the soft toys onto the floor and throw myself onto the sofa. 'Count this!' I tell *The Count*, and then I make a series of rude sounds and gestures at him.

I don't know what's got into me.

But maybe my mother is right. Maybe men *have* used our power over birth as a sword against us, as bars to imprison us? Maybe it *is* all a male conspiracy. Try as I might, though, I'm about as political as Guru Maj's slipper. I phone Sienna for a word of advice but her ansaphone picks up. 'Truth is destiny. Leave a message after the Tibetan prayer bell,' her Bostonian voice trills.

Oh fuck, fuck, fuck.

I decide that what I need to do is to get out of the apartment and clear my head. I send an e-mail to The Jerk, telling him that my column will be late because I'm busy worshipping a Nepalese slipper. Then I head outside and start walking towards the Barnes and Noble bookshop on 82nd on a mission to buy Topsy's book. Mark already owns a well-leafed copy but it seems like a symbolic gesture to actually purchase it myself.

My heels being so high, though, I take a cab across the park and overtip the driver who contravenes every New York cab convention in terms of odour, cleanliness, incense burning and grasp of the English language.

I'm lining up to purchase *I'll Have Mine On The Rocks!* when, flicking through the pages, I notice that it is dedicated to me. 'To Eggnog, my one true love'.

Tears well up in my eyes. I feel confused and alone. The guy at the register asks me if I'm alright and I start to cry uncontrollably until a security guard leads me outside and tells me to beat it.

Walking back across the park, my attitude towards my mother begins to soften. Now that I've had a close shave myself, I can see that it can't be easy being a mother. I fend off the Korean massage squad lying in wait for customers on the 65th Transverse, then I find a bench and sit down to read.

I've read the first chapter by the time a homeless woman, going by the unlikely name of Gin, sits beside me and strikes up a conversation about the messiah. She asks if I'd like to invite Jesus into my heart, but I tell her that I worship a Nepalese slipper and send her packing.

Back at the apartment building, a crowd of pinched faced women with small dogs and snappy voices have assembled in the lobby to discuss the Mayor's latest plan for their safety. It's only been a day, but I miss the Village. I console myself with some muesli (Mark doesn't do cereal) and last week's copy of the *Village Voice*.

Mark comes home from work late, smelling of beer. He empties a Saks bag full of soft toys in peaches, strawberries and baby blues on the bed.

He means the gesture to be ironic. As in, these are so *not* the kind of toys our son or daughter will play with, hell no. He means for me to say, 'Oh Mark, gross!' He means for me to chuckle lightly but my emotions are very labile at the moment and I laugh hysterically. Actually, I laugh so hard that he has to restrain me.

'Are you okay?' he asks, clearly dubious.

'Fine, just um—'

'Hormones?' he suggests.

'Yes, that's it. It's those wretched hormones. I don't know why they don't simply remove them like tonsils. They cause so much heartache and misery to millions. And what do they really do?'

He looks troubled so I go to take a bath. (With the door locked.) When I return all clean and warm, hiding my tampon cord by wearing PJs, I pretend to find his cuddly toy display on the bed sweet and sort of overdo it. I gooh and gah like those insane nannies you see in the park, trying to prove that they're not about to murder their charges.

I think Mark's a bit horrified but he doesn't say so. In fact he suggests sex, which normally would be first thing on my mind too, but instead I tell him that sleeping in the bed is giving me backache and move out to the living room sofa. God-Boy doesn't try too hard to talk me out of it. I guess he presumes this is all part of the mystery of gestation. I go to bed early and read *I'll Have Mine On The Rocks!*.

Topsy outlines her theory on how men have envied the womb since the begining of time. The ability of women to grow a life inside them terrifies men, and this is why they have conspired to oppress us. I wrap the quilt around me tightly and begin to panic.

Is Mark trying to oppress me? He did restrain me over my cuddly toy outburst earlier.

I read on. The next chapter deals with cultures in which women are shut out of the tribal area during their menstruation. I think of Mark sleeping snugly in the triple-sprung comfort of his mattress and begin to question his motives for allowing me to sleep on this sofa.

I read into the early hours of the morning about how men have belittled women by making them ashamed of their bodies, by making them feel that their only worth can be found through giving birth to male children or through being sex slaves. Although actually, I was quite happy being Mark's sex slave.

When he leaves for work, I sneak back into the bed for a nap. My back is killing me. The new pastel-hued soft toys mock me. Even after I shove them under the bed I can hear them taunting me. They scream out that there is no child inside me, and make shrieking sounds like Chuckie in *Childsplay*.

I spend the day in bed reading *I'll Have Mine On The Rocks!*. The Jerk phones and leaves a curt message on the ansaphone suggesting that, slipper or no slipper, he wants my column on time, and what's more, my last one lacked, er, what was the word? Oh yes, that's right, 'lustre'. He demands more single-girl oomph!

The game is up. I can't fake it as a carefree single girl anymore. I haven't been to an opening in months. I haven't weighed myself recently or eaten chocolate in bed. I've even started to eat muesli. I am losing the skills that make me, well . . . me, basically.

I make a promise to myself that I will tell Mark the truth. I will pack my bags, return the Guru Maj slipper to Sienna and move back to my apartment on Hudson. It is time to regain the status quo and my single-girl existence.

Unforeseeably, my plan is sabotaged when Mark

arrives home early with a new dress for me – a black sheath by Prada – and tells me that we are going to a party. We'd been invited weeks ago but we'd both forgotten about it in the excitement of my imagined pregnancy.

He sweeps me into his arms as if I weigh as little as a feather. I can see how lucky I am to have found a guy prepared to lift me with such a show of effortlessness. There is a tricky moment when he carries me off to the bedroom and shows a desire to make love to me. I explain primly that it might not be safe to have sex at this stage of my pregnancy.

I despise myself for lying, but not enough to change course. 'We don't want to . . . dislodge anything,' I blurt out gruesomely.

This statement pretty much puts a pin in his erection. Not even the boisterous libido of a God-Boy wants to get mixed up with the dislodging of an unborn foetus.

Later, as I apply my makeup, I chastise my reflection for using my non-existent baby as an excuse to avoid one of my favourite pastimes. Mark seems pensive as he dresses, unlike his normally chatty evening self, full of anecdotal discourse and humour about his day and his cases.

'I think it's time you saw a doctor,' he tells me as

he finishes shaving. 'Just to get check that there is nothing, you know, wrong.'

I look at him and see him flush. There is something wrong, I want to scream. Something very, very, very wrong. Like the fact that I'm not even pregnant. I feel my face redden and say nothing.

'Not that I'm suggesting there is or anything,' he adds hastily, in a chivalrous effort to reassure me. 'Why would there be?'

Why indeed?

He grabs me and holds my face in his hands. I try to look away as he studies my face with concern. It's as if he is looking right into my uterus, probing like a surgeon into the empty cavern of my lie.

CHAPTER TWELVE

It's official. Most guys in relationships think girls over-play the importance of truth. Truth is dangerous, a great principle, but hard to apply in practice. Most guys would prefer truth to be used only by trained professionals who can accurately gauge the consequences.

If aimed incorrectly, guys point out, the truth can even be fatal, and some guys are concerned that girls are getting trigger happy — firing truth indiscriminately at anyone and anything without counting the cost.

Extract from the 'New York Girl' column of Anna Denier

Anna

When I was still in the casual sex market, I would enter a party like the one I am entering tonight, and graze over the various herds of males with my eyes, like a cheetah scanning for the tasty, weak one. The one that could be brought down in the course of the evening with a minimum amount of chase. The one who wouldn't get all desperate and needy when I kicked him out at three am when I wanted the whole of my bed back. But all that is behind me now. The ordeal of being single rests on the shoulders of other girls, and looking at the men at this party my sense of relief is total.

I can't lie – at least I can, but I'm not going to – this is the party from hell. I know it's only going to get worse from the moment I curl up on an oversized white sofa. I am nursing my big fat lie, not to mention a big fat bottle of whisky. After tenderly nestling me amongst the cushions, Mark takes his leave, telling me that he is going onto the balcony to smoke a celebratory cigar with a few of the guys.

That's why I need this bottle of whisky.

In her book, Topsy talks about pregnancy being a potent symbol of men's virility. I try telling myself that Mark is drawn to the symbolism rather than the kid aspect, but I'm not convinced.

Watching him disappear amongst the party crowd, my heart lurches with love. He is looking especially cool tonight in a casual Armani four-button suit, which fits his body perfectly. Underneath, he's wearing a grey T-shirt that exposes the tiniest bit of his scapular bone. But the tiniest bit is enough.

Alone on the sofa in this room of semi-hostile faces, I want to shrink up Alice in Wonderland-like and disappear. I feel fragile and brittle like a china doll who deserves to be smashed. I am nursing my bottle like a baby, and I know it isn't a good look for a supposedly pregnant girl but I am riding my anti-Madonna image intentionally. I am hoping someone will out me because, let's face it, the only way the truth will come out is if someone ties a string to it, attaches it to a door handle and slams the door with a serious degree of force.

Left to my own devices I could lie about this pregnancy forever. Even after my due date comes and goes, I'd continue to lie. They can put me in hospital and cut me open before I'll tell. Exposure is my only hope. As I take another slug of whisky, my whole demeanour is screaming, 'Expose me! Go on, drag me by the scruff of my Prada (only not too roughly, obviously), and shake me about like the obscene Jezebel that I am!'

I couldn't have imagined that *not* being pregnant would be this hard. I've even started flirting with the possibility of actually getting pregnant. I could do it. After my period is over, I could have wild, unprotected sex and there is every chance that I really will conceive. This would certainly offer a way out of telling the truth.

Am I really considering this as an option? Am I *really* that hard up? Pah-lease. I spent yesterday worshipping a slipper, didn't I?

In her book, my mother also discusses how women have, at various times throughout history, been forced to conceal their pregnancy until after wedlock. I'm kicking myself now for not concealing my pregnancy until I was actually pregnant. In the taxi on the way to the party, I was reading about how society has forced women to adhere to monogamy while accepting men's philandering as natural. The whole system geared to guarantee the husband's paternity.

'Don't men stink?' Topsy asks the reader. I sniffed the air around Mark as the cab inched its way down Park. Givenchy, I decide as I read on.

Due to their economic dependency, society has used women's reproductive powers to enslave them. In the nineteenth century women were frequently reduced to securing marriage proposals based on false claims of pregnancy.

Pondering this point now, as I watch the party start to swing, it strikes me as bizarre that in the twenty-first century I am considering covering up *not* being pregnant by getting pregnant. All so I won't look foolish. The soulful voice of Lauryn Hill starts up.

I am pathetic and low. Knowing this, I take another slug from the bottle and practically choke.

As I scan the room again, I quite fancy taking a package holiday to oblivion. Instead, I take another slug as I focus on a group of guys by the corner bookcase. My boyfriend's long haul friends. I've met them all several times, enough to be sure I loathe them, and for them to be certain I'm not good enough for their friend.

They've been with him from the playground and are planning a long slog to the grave. They are men with an eye on the future, whereas I am a girl with an eye on the latest fad, or the latest invite to slide under my door.

Their conversation involves a lot of back-slapping

and loud discussion on the merits of the feminist backlash currently sweeping North America. And when I say loudly, I'm playing it down. These guys must assume that anyone in a three-mile radius is hanging on their every word.

'Even women are sick of feminists now.'

Canned laughter.

'Look at that mad Topsy Denier,' Dome Head declares.

'Shhh, she's sitting over there.' Nudges and lowered voices.

'Girl-power, post-girl-power, call it what you want, it is all so over!'

They all agree heartily, voices raised again.

'What's the problem with being a guy, anyway? What have we done that's so bad?' they ask – only not me directly. Obviously not, because I could have delivered a pretty compelling discourse on that question. To me feminism is kind of like my Billy Joel. Other kids had to listen to Billy Joel, I had to listen to Germaine Greer and Gloria Steinem. Like all kids my age, I closed my ears whenever Greer or Steinem were playing, but in a kind of retro-sentimental way I'd grown fond of the girls over the years.

I take another gulp of whisky. I really need to get smashed. Really, really, really gone. I check the guys out again as I wonder how so many deeply unfuckable men have managed to group themselves together without even seeing the irony of the situation. They are like a clearing house of uglies. A never-do-well clump of guys who have kindly sorted themselves into a group, like a pile of smelly socks. Which is convenient after a fashion when you think about it. Every girl on Manhattan can relax. 'Phew!' they can sigh, 'At least I know where *not* to focus my attentions this evening.'

To top it off, The Uglies have chosen the tomes of Brett Easton Ellis's *American Psycho*, Nick Hornby's *High Fidelity*, Martin Amis's *The Information*, Jack Kerouac's everything, and several other assorted semantic texts on buddyism as their conversational backdrop. Such contrivance is not beyond the scope of these guys – you just have to sniff their cologne to know that.

The question begged – how did Mark get mixed up with a bunch of friends like these? He's known them all his life, that's how. And he isn't the sort of guy to ditch people. Not like me; at the first sign of boredom I cry, 'Man overboard', and run. Mark is loyal and true and I feel ashamed to even be in his orbit.

His friends all think that he is making a big mistake with me; even he knows they think this. Well, they told him actually. But he thought they would all come round in time, once they got to know me. He said I had got it all wrong. They loved me really.

(That was why I was alone on the couch, right?) The problem was, they'd been so attached to his last girlfriend, Rebecca. Really talented, undeniably pretty, Homecoming Queen, blonde, perfect, lot of fun to hang out with blah, blah, blah. You know the type. Fingers-down-the-back-of-your-throat cute.

'Real' was the word everyone used to describe her, as in, Rebecca was so real. Real? Apart from not being pregnant, not being real is my main problem. I'm not in the least bit real. From the tips of my blonde hair to my artificial cleavage, I am the sort of girl who can't run down to the store without some sort of artifice, even if it is only a cigarette on the lower lip and a pair of dark sunglasses. If I bother to get dressed at all, I go all the way. Casual and natural are not my forte.

'Wait till they get to know you,' Mark is always insisting. 'They can't help but love you.' It is his dream. Like the way Russians dream that Anastasia is still running around Paris, planning a comeback tour. I dream of becoming a size six. 'Dreams keep us going,' I try and tell him. 'But sadly, they rarely come true.'

At that moment, a Creedence Clearwater Revival hit from the seventies starts up on the stereo. A few girls and one very silly guy, who is actually wearing a cravat (and meaning it), start dancing on the Moroccan rug. A quick check on the looks they are getting, especially from other girls, confirms my hunch that they are making a big mistake.

Even a girl like me with a knack for doing the wrong thing can see that this is not the party to get your rocks off at. This is v. much the party at which to keep your inner self to your self. Even a quiet multiple personality was more welcome than self-expression in this West End Ave. apartment.

I can't help thinking that *I Heard It On The Grapevine* is an ironic reference to a persistent rumour that has been doing the rounds of Mark's friends' parties, namely that I had become pregnant on purpose. Perish the thought. Me, willingly get pregnant? Me, allow an alien to inhabit my body? Me, wilfully undertake to put on thirty pounds? *NOT!*

But my hell is just beginning. Now I can see that the uglies and the dancers are the last thing I should be focusing on. Like a big spider (albeit in a Donna Karan frock), Rebecca, in a puff of Versace and a swish of natural blondeness, has just sat down.

Beside *me*.

CHAPTER THIRTEEN

Ex-girlfriends are the enemy, always. The nemesis of any relationship. Ex-girlfriends are anti-girlfriends, no matter what they tell you. And any guy who trusts his ex and asks you to do the same is either missing something (i.e. the break-up) or concealing something (i.e. the lack of closure).

Extract from the 'New York Girl' column of Anna Denier

Anna

'I saw you looking at those guys. Not *all* Mark's friends are such jerks,' Rebecca tells me as she slumps down on the sofa. 'Those guys over by the books are—'

'Er . . . jerks?' I offer.

She laughs, one of those real throaty laughs. 'I don't know why we still hang out with them.' I nod as she rolls her eyes in mock horror. 'I hope you don't think we're *all* like that?'

I smile stiffly rather than admit that, actually, I very much *do*. I can see that she is only trying to be nice, but really I don't want to talk to anyone. And more than anyone, I don't want to talk to Mark's ex, even if she is the nicest, funniest, coolest girl at the party. Even if she is engaged to someone else now. Exes are exes for a reason, and I distrust Mark's lingering friendship with her, even if it is a really hip and healthy thing to do these days.

'I can see why you're doing it,' she continues, sipping on her wine. At first I think she's reading my mind. Radiant, with her cute, long blonde hair (natural), her perfect nose (natural), and her peaches and cream complexion, I really, really hate natural and I hate, hate, her. That is to say I hate her very much indeed. Despise her even. I can't help myself. I can't look at her perfect bee-sting lips and not imagine Mark kissing them. I bet she's a really great kisser too. Better than me with my fag on my lip.

'What?' I ask, expecting to be accused of something heinous.

'Getting pregnant.'

(Gulp)

'I really wish I could just get pregnant like that. But Rob would kill me.'

'Pretty harsh,' I say, although not altogether the worst case scenario I secretly decide.

Rebecca giggles. 'Mark always talks about how funny you are,' she remarks, taking another sip of her drink.

Sienna had lent me her *Voodoo for Idiots* book and I had actually read the first step-by-step spell for beginners on the loo.

Fashion a wax doll in the image of your enemy, it instructed. (Well, what could be easier?) What came after that though? I try and remember, but that's the trouble with reading on the toilet – there's never the time.

'I really want to have kids, more than I'd ever admit to Rob. I can already hear my biological clock ticking away and I'm only twenty-nine.'

'Maybe you could flick the snooze button,' I say.

She doesn't laugh, though, and I notice that her eyes are transfixed on something in the middle distance. 'I know I could put my eggs on ice, but that's not the point. I don't really want to be a mother in my forties.' She touches my arm lightly. I look at her neatly manicured hand. She's making an effort to bond with me. Mark probably had a word with her or something because the rest of his friends are treating me like a leper. I try and smile but my facial muscles double cross me and it comes off sort of smarmy and false as I notice her huge breasts and real cleavage.

Voodoo for Idiots, I remember now. I need to get some of Rebecca's hair (easy), saliva (doubtful) and menstrual blood (v. hard indeed). A few verses of mumbo jumbo and a bit of incense and I could cast her out of my life forever.

'You have lovely hair,' I remark.

'Gee, thanks.'

'Um, can I have some?' I ask hopefully.

'What?'

'Some hair. Just a small sample to . . . to . . . to remember you by.'

She giggles so I go for broke.

'Or saliva perhaps?' She giggles some more. 'Saliva would be very handy. Only if you don't mind—'

'I'm terrified of turning forty and feeling desperate. You know that point in a woman's life when all she really wants is kids?' I'm thinking how I don't really when she nudges me.

I nudge her back. 'I'm more or less desperate all the time,' I tell her. 'Driven by fear and neuroses and deep-seated problems with my mother. So, by the way, when is your period due?'

Rebecca falls about in paroxysms of giggles. 'Sorry, but you are soooo funny.' She points at me as she says this and I feel singled out. I feel like she's laughing *at* me not *with* me. I really wish she wouldn't laugh quite so hard because people are beginning to stare. I wonder what I can do to make her cry. Maybe if I start, good-sport that she is, she'll join in. But she composes herself and starts going on about Topsy's theory on personal fulfilment for women again. 'It's all very well to put your eggs on ice like your mom says in her book, but I still don't want to be an old mother.' She rolls her big green eyes some more. She does that a lot; perhaps it's a condition. In lieu of something to say, I roll my eyes back at her, but after all the whisky I've drunk, it makes me dizzy.

She wrinkles her nose as I wobble a bit, and goes on, 'I simply don't think I'll want to deal with diapers and night feeds at that age. I think you're right to get it over with.'

I am wondering if God-Boy has thought about diapers and night feeds? Or is he imagining that I will deal with that side of parenthood? I begin to feel a little hot under the collar at this idea.

'My problem is I'm scared,' she continues. 'You know my fiancé, Rob?'

I nod without emotion as I pull out a cigarette and stick it on my lower lip. Usually this panics onlookers into saying something along the lines of 'you can't smoke here!' but I'm beyond caring.

'God I hate that term, *fiancé*,' she adds. 'It sounds so—'

'Crap?'

'Yeah.' She grins. 'Anyway, Rob is determined not to have kids until he's in his forties. Which is fine for him, but I already want them. Want them a lot. Do you want a light for that, Anna?'

I shake my head. 'Nah, I just put it there for comfort.'

She smiles at me sweetly and I look at her carefully for the first time. Really look at her.

'I envy you,' she says, suddenly looking into my eyes. 'I try and tell myself that I'm not ready for diapers and night feeds just yet.' Now she really does look like she might cry.

I want to reach out or say something but I don't actually know what to do when your lover's ex-girlfriend gets maudlin. I offer her my bottle of whisky but she waves it away.

'You shouldn't *really* be drinking that, you know,' she tells me.

My shame rises up my neck like a barcode.

'Shall I take this?' she suggests firmly, prizing the bottle from my hands. 'Honestly Anna, we should get together sometime, just you and me. Away from this lot.' She waves her arm around the room dismissively.

And despite my vow to hate her, I nod. 'I'd like that,' I say, suspecting that, despite my self-preserving instincts, I would like Rebecca.

'I love your outfit, by the way. You look great, hardly showing at all,' she remarks as she glides away and dissolves into the crowd. It's always the 'hardlys' that hurt the most.

In search of water, I stick the cigarette back on my lip and make my way through the huddled groups to the drinks table. Mark comes in from the balcony as I'm about to take my first sip. He looks frightened. 'Are you okay? What's that you're drinking?' he demands to know.

I tell him that it's water.

But he seems far from convinced and tries to take

the glass from me. Too thirsty to give it up that easily, I pull the glass away and it spills all over his trousers. I look at the stain as it spreads around his groin, but he suddenly takes me in his arms and tells me that he loves me.

I apologise about the water. 'Forget it,' he says, drawing me tightly into his chest. 'I shouldn't have been so suspicious. Someone said they saw you drinking and I was worried.'

The wet patch feels cold against my body and I pull away. 'Was it Rebecca? Did Rebecca say something?' I am suddenly righteous and ready to defend myself on all charges, true or false.

'Rebecca? No, it was one of the guys, but that's not the point. Why? Were you drinking?' He looks suspicious.

I breathe in and look him in the eye. 'Mark, I have to tell you something. I should have told you yesterday. I meant to, only I could see how happy you were.'

He repeats the word 'were', his lightning-fast intellect grasping the significance of the past tense immediately.

'It's about the baby.'

But he's looking at the wet patch on his pants, which is pretty large. It looks as if he's wet himself, which can't thrill him. The music stops and if I'd had a larger brain capacity I would have noticed that everyone has gone quiet, as if they were listening to something. Listening to us.

'You're wet,' I announce, trying to stall the inevitable as he leads me into the empty kitchen.

'Forget me. What did you want to tell me?' He shuts the door. 'About the baby?'

There is no way to avoid the issue now. I've given too much away, although perhaps not telling him and then getting pregnant isn't such a lame idea. Not that I want a child, but at this moment I would drink a cup of hemlock to avoid the task to which I am committed.

These are the thoughts swimming through my head when Dome Head bursts into the kitchen. Sighting my illicit cigarette he tells me grimly that I can't smoke in Rebecca and Rob's apartment.

'That's okay, it's just resting. Tired, you know. I was just resting it on my lip while I load up my hypodermic with heroin. Would you be a sweetie and find me a tourniquet?'

Mark steps in to defuse the situation. 'Er . . . we are a bit busy at the moment, George. I think we need a minute on our own.'

George can't oblige him fast enough, but as he closes the swing doors into the kitchen I feel suddenly claustrophobic.

'He's right, you should stop smoking,' Mark mutters. 'Can't be good for the baby, can it?'

'There isn't going to be a baby, Mark.' And then I add, 'I'm sorry.'

There, I've said it.

CHAPTER FOURTEEN

The Upper East Side is not a place, it is a state of mind. It is a state of mind where you feel secure and safe and liberal and respectable all at once. There are no edges to fall off on the Upper East Side and all the corners are rounded so that children can't hurt themselves. You can never be too thin or too made up on the Upper East Side, any more than your dogs can be too small or your shoes too European.

Extract from the 'New York Girl' column of Anna Denier

Anna

Two weeks later, Mark is still inconsolable about the loss of my pregnancy. I can feel his eyes on me sometimes, accusatory eyes that say, you never wanted this baby, anyway. Did you?

I can't believe he is this distressed over the loss of a baby that technically never existed. Babies, as far as I am concerned, are like fancy dinner parties, fluffy towels, clever recipes and wallpaper – something couples use to menace single girls.

No one actually wants babies, I'm convinced of that much. It's just a load of hype, an advertiser's fancy, a means of selling products. We are made to feel like we want babies by vested commercial interests who pressure us into it. I try to explain this to Mark in the hope that he will see reason.

'So what you're saying is that no one actually likes babies? All those couples going through the expense and torture of IVF treatment are being conned? Is that what you're saying?'

He hasn't actually admitted that he is devastated

but there is a simmering atmosphere about him lately, like Vesuvius. I'm thinking about calling a state of Relationship Emergency and letting the Thought Police or even the Emotional Red Berets take over. I'd like to think that something as simple as a few jack-boots, SWAT teams and automatic weapons could sort out this mess. But I doubt it.

We've started niggling each other over chores and other dumb stuff. He doesn't seem like such a fantasy guy now. Unless we are talking extremely-sicko-domestic-drudge fantasy. I am in a *real* relationship with a *real* guy and I'm not sure I'm equipped for it. I liked it better when everything I did and said made him puff with pleasure and laugh affectionately.

So why don't I want to live anywhere other than within this relationship? I do what my father used to do with my mother and try to block my unhappiness out. Jack used to wear earplugs when Topsy cried after discovering one of his affairs. That was before she realised there were hundreds of them lurking all over San Francisco like nests of spiders. Then his earplugs offered about as much protection as a calf-skin shield against a Saturday Night Special.

I have even more unpleasant chores to tackle – The Jerk, basically. He's asked me to 'fluff up' my column. Fluff? Isn't that something you excavate from a belly button? I ask Mark but he's too busy brooding. I start typing my latest obscene e-mail to The Jerk; I don't intend to send it, but writing these letters soothes me. Dear The Jerk, I type. You are a one-celled organism, a Luddite of very little character, and I would appreciate it ever so much if you would kindly stick your head in a bucket. And so on and so forth.

Mark is wandering quietly about the large apartment when suddenly he picks up our earlier discussion with so much vigour, I accidentally push SEND.

I am doomed. Reasons to hurl myself off the Empire State Building are steadily mounting up. Now, not only will The Jerk know what I want him to do with his head and a bucket, but he will know that I call him The Jerk. The secret is out.

I must have missed a fair bit of Mark's no doubt beautifully prepared argument while I unsuccessfully tried to retrieve the e-mail from the cyber-world.

'. . . who knows,' he is suggesting, when I finally tune in to him again. 'Maybe your desire for babies is in retrograde?'

'Retrograde?' I repeat, giving him the opportunity to retract the word.

'All right, not retrograde. I'm just suggesting that your need for babies might be, well, dormant or something. Hibernating. Is that possible, do you think? You don't want kids now, but what about the future?'

I can tell by the look on his face that he thinks he's on to something.

'A desire for babies isn't like a virus or a cancer cell,' I point out. 'If we are going to speak in analogies, wanting a baby is more like having a free radical floating around a body of healthy don't-want-children cells. Like a meteorite waiting to impact.'

He looks sceptical. 'How can you be so certain of how you'll feel in ten or even twenty years' time?' he demands.

'Because I've had over twenty years' experience of *not* wanting children,' I reply, as a dancing baby screen save mysteriously appears on my monitor. 'Where did this bloody baby thing come from?' I yell.

Mark looks at me smugly. 'Oh that. I put it on for you. Downloaded it for you while you were sleeping. I thought you'd like it. You know, it's the one from *Ally McBeal*, with that music, you know. "Unka-chucka-unka-chuka!!!! I can't stop this feeling, deep inside of me",' he sings, before noticing my frown.

The one feeling I can't stop is the feeling that I am under attack from everyone and everything. Even my own computer is against me. How did the baby issue take over my life like this? I don't want kids. Not now, probably not ever. My flirtation with putting some eggs on ice was based on a gamble with my future. But I don't want to gamble with Mark's.

'I thought you'd like it.'

He looks so crumpled when I say, 'I so do *not* like it.' He reminds me of those guys that mutter under their breath and hang around Times Square.

I slump over my keyboard miserably. Does having children mean that much to him? Because if it does, I might turn out to be a big, big disappointment.

I wish I had a mother rather than a Topsy to talk about all this stuff with. As the days wear on, Mark seems to be feeling his loss more rather than less. What is the appropriate period of grief for losing a baby you never had? I try to be sympathetic but his disappointment is in conflict with my secret jubilation.

He is so downhearted, and I am so to blame. I do everything I can to bring him out of his shell. I shave my legs, I watch reruns of *Seinfeld* with him and pretend to find Kramer endearingly funny. I even talk about cooking something. As a last resort, I pretend to enjoy the company of his friends, which basically back-fires when one of them rings up and complains that I was patronising him.

Despite all my best efforts, his gloom stretches on for weeks. He couldn't have made me feel worse if he'd proved world starvation was down to me. Girls who say that men don't feel things as deeply as women are wrong. I should know, because I used to be one of those girls before I met Mark. I got it from Topsy.

'Men have all the sensitivity of a worn sock and should be treated accordingly,' my mother famously declared on the *Ed Sullivan Show* – the day I started high school, as it happens. I wasn't asked out once during my senior high years. Guys didn't want to run the risk of getting intimate with a girl who was likely to lose them in the wash.

I hate her for putting my face on her last book, *Kids: Who Needs Them?* Even though the image was all grainy and blurred. Even though the tenet of the book was that no one *needed* children to feel complete, they should *want* them. 'Children should be your heart's desire, not a utility,' was the theme of her discussion. I make a mental note not to leave a copy of *Kids: Who Needs Them?* lying around the apartment.

'Mark is genuinely disappointed,' I tell Topsy when she calls. I'm half hoping for some support.

'Well, of course he is,' she breezes. 'You can't give a man hopes and then dash them, Eggnog.'

I start picking at a gooey bit on my cardigan as she prattles on. 'I imagine he started to feel things he hadn't felt before.'

'Like what, pray tell?'

'Like his DNA,' she explains. 'You know, dynasty things.'

'Dynasty things?' I exclaim. 'And what the hell is a dynasty *thing*?'

'Well, I spoke to his mother and apparently she told him that he could have his old cradle. It's a family heirloom. The family smuggled it out with them from Germany in 1932.'

'You've been speaking to his mother?' I shriek. 'Who gave you the right to start calling his mother?'

'Every woman must write her own rights, Eggnog! And besides, she called me.'

'She hates you,' I inform her, even though I have no hard evidence to substantiate this slur. Just something about the tone his mother used when she said, 'Oh, you're related to that Denier woman? Ah yes. That explains a lot.'

'She's been charming for someone who hates me. She wants me to address her self-development group in Greenwich.'

'You're not going to are you?' I ask darkly.

'I might,' she sniffs. 'Maybe you should come with me, Eggnog. You might learn something. I must admit that I concur with Alicia, you are being too harsh with Mark.'

'Who's Alicia?'

'His mother. It's a bit selfish of you not to know

the name of the poor boy's mother, Eggnog. A few weeks ago you were promising her grandchildren,' she sighs, as if I've somehow let everyone down.

'She was introduced to me as Mrs Weinberg,' I point out, with a bit of an edge in my voice. 'And on top of that, Mark is not poor, not remotely. The truth is, he can't stay miserable forever.'

'There isn't always a time limit on misery,' Topsy points out, as if she knows this from personal experience.

PS: as if Topsy has ever had a day's misery in her life.

'Gosh, you're so wise, Topsy. I never knew that about you,' I tell her, my voice laced with sarcasm. I am bloody annoyed with her for taking Mark's side. 'Anyway, we'd never even discussed children,' I add. 'And on top of that I don't want any, so there. It's for the best!'

'The best for whom?' she asks.

But I haven't got an answer, just a lot of questions.

She hangs up, leaving me feeling guiltier than ever. Even though I had never, at any point, suggested that I was certain of my pregnancy, I am being made to feel callous and hurtful. All because I hadn't accidentally conceived. Now even my own mother, the doyen of a woman's right to choose, is down on me. I check there is a cigarette on my lip and light it.

I love Mark, but I'm not going to be made to feel like I've cheated him out of a dynasty merely because I had a late period. Something rises up inside, something strong and wilful and determined. It's time that the people who profess to love me recognise me as the person I really am.

I start my new life by taking off the cashmere cardigan that Mark's sister had given me when I'd complained about how cold the air conditioning was. Then I begin to pack. I write Mark a note explaining how we both want different things and how it is all for the best that we split, blah, blah, blah.

By the time Mark returns to his Upper East Side apartment that evening, I am happily back on Hudson, arguing with my super about the heating. Well, maybe not that happy. It is freezing but he says we aren't having the heating on before November. Then he starts talking about the Gulf War, as in, did I know he was there?

I try to escape up the stairs, but Sienna, hearing the commotion, storms out of her apartment wearing a purple turban and a caftan and demands Guru Maj's slipper back.

'Anna, you've got to give me back the slipper, now!'

I start apologising profusely for keeping the slipper so long, but she cuts me short.

'It's not what it seems.'

'Why, what's happened?'

'It's been cursed by a black magician.'

When I hand it over I spot that the odour-eater I'd placed inside has dissolved. And maybe I've just been hanging around Sienna too long but I actually think this is significant and that she might be on to something.

Pushing these thoughts from my mind, I unpack and try to do some work, but no matter what button I push, I can't get rid of the dancing baby screen save.

CHAPTER FIFTEEN

I have never been the world's greatest dater. I am too hyper, too expectant, too analytical. Courtship is for patient types, people who can string their lust out.

I have never strung anything out, apart from toffee. That's my problem, I need to know where something is going before I agree to join in. I need to know that the fairytale ending is in place before I engage. And that isn't how love actually works.

Extract from the 'New York Girl' column of Anna Denier

Anna

I'm slumped on the couch back at Hudson with my toys. I feel as though I am stuck inside a serialised nightmare of my own making. I don't feel like going out or even working. Turn the page, I urge myself. Your relationship with Mark had no future. It had failure written into it from the start. He wants kids, you don't. It was bound to blow up soon, anyway. But philosophy was never my strong point.

Anyway, he called the night I moved out.

He didn't phone but arrived at my door in person, bearing champagne, oysters and yoghurt – the staples of our love. For some reason – which I am still going over in my head – I slammed the door in his face, thereby setting a pattern in our relationship. He rings, I hang up. I have to be strong. It would be so v. easy to get back with Mark. But I'd be fooling us both. His longing for children would still be there, like a tripwire in our future.

Over the past month, I have hung up on him more than two dozen times. Most of those hang ups took place in the first week. Since then, I have been waiting for him to call so that I can hang up again. I can watch the phone not ringing for hours now; I've developed it into an art form. I call-screen so thoroughly that people are starting to think I'm ubercool. I've had a lot of practice over the years with Topsy, I guess.

Sienna has been totally supportive. We talk for hours. She comes down most evenings and makes disgustingly evil herbal brews that are really good for obscure emotional states like malfeasance and turgidity. I don't ask.

She tells me about her lousy love life and, strangely, that does more towards healing me than anything else could because it makes *my* love life sound as racy and enviable as a Jackie Collins novel. She's also the only person I know in New York who hasn't really got close to Mark, so I can talk frankly without her flying into rhapsodies about him and making me feel worse.

'Truth is destiny,' she repeats in that inimitable way of hers as she drinks her bitter herbal teas. 'Just cut back on high-karma situations and you'll be fine.'

If only it was that easy.

'But Mark *is* my high-karma situation,' I wail, fixing her with a don't-you-dare glare lest she start on her 'truth is destiny' rubbish again.

Later that night, Mark rings. 'I need to reclaim my own life,' I explain, knowing I sound like a bad line from one of my mother's books.

'Can't we even date?' he asks reasonably.

'We never dated,' I remind him. 'We never even had That Conversation. We lived together ever since I fell on you in the men's restroom at the Tribeca Grill.'

'Oh yeah, that's right,' he agrees, sounding worryingly uncertain about how we got together.

I remember that night even if he doesn't. Vividly. Even the bits I didn't really remember the morning after are as clear as one of Sienna's crystals now. I used my imagination to fill in the blanks and turned it into a night of utter romance.

We talk generally like civilised adults about films and art exhibitions, both of us making a pretence of being madly social when I can tell he's moping as much as me.

The difference is I have to concentrate on my voice to stop it sounding emotionally desolate, whereas he speaks reasonably and with assurance, as if he scripted the conversation earlier. I toy with the idea that he had his secretary write his speech for him but I don't care; I let his voice pour from the phone into my mind like one of Sienna's meditation tapes. A telephone relationship would suit me perfectly. I could be like Andy Warhol.

He brings the talk round to us seeing each other again. 'Maybe our *not* dating is why things went wrong. Maybe we *should* date.' he suggests. 'Maybe that was our problem.'

'Gee,' I say, trying out my new Warhol persona, but I crumble almost immediately. Despite my fantasy of limiting myself to phone relationships, the sound of Mark's voice isn't enough. In fact, it's only broken my resolve to not see him again. The way he pauses before he speaks, the way I can hear him smiling, all contrive to make me feel out of control. I stick my cigarette back on my lower lip. He sounds even sexier on the phone, sexier and more desirable. I've never been much of a resolution keeper. It's pointless to fight it. With all the spinal column of a worm, I agree to try the dating thing, but tell him that I can't offer any guarantees. As if all the cards are in my hands or something.

He agrees, suggesting a restaurant on the Upper West Side that we've never been to.

I agree back, suggesting a time.

He agrees with me.

We are being so agreeable, we sound like strangers

answering a lonely hearts ad in the *Village Voice*. 'Just as long as you know where you stand, though – where we both stand,' I tell him, as if I am twenty-something-with-big-bust (I wish) and he is thirty-something-career-guy-with-prospects.

'There's no pressure, Anna. The last thing I want to do is pressure you. We're both free agents here, you know, under no obligations.'

'Free? Agents?' Oh, not the free agent thing. What is this, a James Bond movie? I don't want to date him as a free agent. I want to have a wild, devastatingly committed relationship with him, long conversations into the night, kissing till our lips dry out. I want all of him, all the time. I want the future to be with him.

'We can take it one step at a time.'

'Isn't that the motto for sobriety in Alcoholics Anonymous?' I quip, and I hear him smiling on the other end.

Up till now, I have only ever wanted to live in the moment, but now I have an urge to plan. I am jumping up on my tip-toes, looking out for what's over the horizon. I want to plan wasting time with Mark, stretched out on crumpled sweaty sheets while a Chopin CD plays in the flat opposite. I'm so over 'Smack My Bitch Up'. So over.

I've moved away from all my cherished teen

positions. I am a twenty-something and I want a twenty-something's life. I don't want fragments of his time. Stolen evenings in stiff restaurants with wannabe-actress waitresses hovering for a tip so they can pay the cab fare to their next audition. I want it all. I want the star role.

I even want the boring bits when we don't have anything to say and we're all orgasmed out, stretched out and sated in front of the television, planning a future, paying bills, taking out savings plans, chatting away about mortgages. (Okay, now I'm just taking the piss.)

I agree to meet him at Cafe Des Artistes on the Upper West Side on Thursday. I am sure he knows how much I'm dreading meeting him in this gravely conservative venue. At least I hope he does.

I also hope he knows that I will feel uncomfortable with the dating thing and that we will both end up at my apartment scooping orgasms off our bodies into the dawn. But what if he doesn't know any of these things? What if he thinks I'm actually *capable* of the dating thing? Capable of patience and casual relationships? No, surely he wouldn't be that stupid?

Maybe I should send him an e-mail.

See, that is me all over. I am always leaping ahead of a situation. Part of me wants to break into his apartment while he's at work today and move my things back here. Part of me wants to cancel the date out of fear that I will leap too far, too soon and scare him. Like those streakers that dived out at policemen and over cricket pitches in the seventies.

I am afraid of what I feel and what I will have to give up if I let these feelings have their way. This last month without him has been a twilight zone of pizza and ice-cream and not opening mail. I am not sorry to see it end but I know that I am like a heroin addict who has been straight for a few months.

And now I am about to have a taste.

I know that I will be addicted again within a week, and worse than knowing that is the knowing that I will have to go into detox again. Because no matter how much I love him, Mark is not good for me and I am not good for him. I learnt that during my detox period. He wants children and I don't. I should have said no. I should stay here alone in my apartment, in detox, forever.

Otherwise I'll end up on the school run in Connecticut, scattering cushions in my spare time.

Gee.

On top of the burden of missing Mark, I have the Topsy issue to cope with. She has taken to ringing me daily just to spook me. My mother has always been sporadic in her attentions, but Mark has seemingly inflamed her interest in me.

Sienna, bless her heart, is now the sanest person in my world. She's making me an elixir to lower my karma levels tonight. I only hope it works.

CHAPTER SIXTEEN

The past is best left in the past.

It's a space–time continuum thing. By moving matter from one time zone to another, a lot of stuff can get lost in translation. For previous experiences management, I prefer the selective delete method.

Keep what you want and leave the rest. Just like when you go through your photo albums and tear up your fat stage. In one afternoon, it's as if it never happened. Ex-boyfriends? Only talk about the ones with impressive characteristics. (Delete Chuck the spotty one who picked his nose when he thought you weren't looking.) Counting up calories consumed in a week? Who counts Orky bars?

Extract from the 'New York Girl' column of Anna Denier

Mark

'Do you think the reason we fucked up so badly was because we never had That Conversation?' I ask her for the fiftieth time that afternoon.

Rebecca's been stirring sugar into her tea for the last five minutes. Washington, her ginger cat, is pawing the back of the chair on which I'm sitting, and every so often one of his claws hits my skull. Like now.

'Shoot!'

'Washington!' Bec warns. 'Be a good boy.'

'It's fine,' I say, leaning forward as if to avoid another laceration. 'I'm just tired. I'm not sleeping, see. Not since Anna . . . Oh God.' I put my head in my hands and moan.

Rebecca's always been good for tea and sympathy. But not today. 'Come on Mark, get a grip,' she snaps, finally laying down her spoon. She's always taken sugar in her tea. *Real* sugar as opposed to that fake shit I've seen some girls use. Watching them empty that stuff into their beverage really cringes guys out.

Like taking a girl on a date and watching her eat half a salad and say she's full. Yeah, like anyone believes that.

'Seriously, Mark, you've got to pull yourself together on this,' she persists, speaking more gently this time, as if to Washington.

But I know as well as Bec that I lost my grip on my relationship with Anna the day I started. The day I started what, you wonder?

The day I started lying.

I put my head in my hands again. Washington jumps into Bec's lap and starts rubbing her body on her chest. Rebecca has serious tits. I forget that sometimes. I used to be obsessed with them once. I drag my gaze away from her chest and look her in the eyes. 'What can I do? I've fucked up Bec.'

'Hey, it's not as if you've lied to her or anything,' she tries to soothe me.

I look at her questioningly. 'I haven't?'

'Not directly.'

'No? What would you call it then?'

'Okay, so you lied.'

'Thanks.'

'Not lied quite, you er . . .'

'Neglected to tell the truth?'

'You concealed stuff.'

'And that's okay? You'd be okay with that if Rob concealed stuff from you?'

'That's different. Stop beating yourself up over it will you?'

'Lying, neglecting, concealing. Whatever you call it, withholding information is as good as lying, Bec. You're a lawyer, you know that.'

She sips her tea. We sit in silence for a while and I listen to Washington's purring. 'I like her,' Bec says quietly, looking into my eyes. She has large green saucer eyes like Washington and I know she means what she says. Unlike me, Rebecca is nothing if not honest. I've always been able to talk to her and I know she won't jerk me around. Bec was never the sort to bend the truth. Although we've not been as close since she got engaged to Rob, Bec's almost one of the guys. As long as you don't look at her tits that is.

'Thanks Bec, that means a lot to me. No one else is too keen on her, that's for sure.'

'You mean your mother?'

'I mean everyone. And she knows it, too.'

'That's crap. Rob really digs her.'

I smile. 'That makes me feel better,' I say, stifling what could easily become a laughing fit. I don't want to tell Rebecca that Anna refers to Rob as Vagina Man (owing to his career as a gynaecologist).

'They're all just jealous,' she adds comfortingly,

mistaking the noises bursting out of me as heartfelt. 'They're a bunch of in-breds, anyway. They're angry because you've dated outside our set, that's all. Give her ten years and they'll think she's one of us,' she teases.

I smile. 'Like red-neck communities in the South you mean?'

'She's gorgeous, she's funny. What, you think they're going to thank you for scoring with a babe like Anna? She's beyond them, that's all.'

'Yeah, well maybe. She's certainly beyond my folks.'

'Pah-lease. You're in trouble when your parents start liking the girls you bring home.'

'They liked you,' I remind her.

We give one another a knowing look, both of us remembering the way my parents tried to manipulate our relationship. We've always laughed together. When we went to Israel ten years ago we used to stay up all night laughing. Shit, was it really that long ago? She had long hair back then. I used to plait it like those dressage horses while we talked. 'I've fucked up big time with Anna and I don't know what to do,' I blurt. My voice is pleading, helpless.

Bec clicks her tongue. 'What do you mean you've fucked up big time? What is it you've done exactly?' she quizzes me, twirling a strand of hair in her finger.

'You mean apart from the lying?' She arches her eyebrows. 'Sorry, the concealing?' I correct, giving her a wry smile. 'There was this whole baby thing. I reacted badly to that.'

'Yeah, what was that all about? I didn't dare ask at the time.'

'Nor did I. I just got sucked along in the slipstream of it all, I guess. When she said she was pregnant, I didn't know what to think.'

'Why didn't you tell her then?'

'I really overdid it, didn't I?'

'*Could* be pregnant. She only ever said she could be pregnant. You were the one who overreacted, remember?'

'Could be, was, whatever. That's because I was scared and fucking out of my mind with fear. I overdid it.'

'Why didn't you tell her afterwards then?'

'Talking to her would involve telling her the truth and telling her the truth would mean—'

Rebecca made a face. 'Fuck.'

'Yeah, fuck.'

She comes over to me, squats on her haunches and holds my arm. 'Hey, it's over now. Let it go. Make it up to her, admit what a jerk you were, get down on your knees and beg her to take you back.'

'Maybe you're right, maybe it's that easy,' I say, in a

voice that means I don't think that at all. Washington starts clawing the back of the chair again.

'Should I call her?' she asks.

'You?'

I watch her long fingers still twirling the hair around her face. 'I was going to call her anyway. We arranged to get together when she was here that night. I wouldn't mind hanging out with her, doing girl stuff. Hey, I could have a talk with her about you.'

I freeze. 'Maybe not, Bec,' I say stiffly.

She giggles as she pulls Washington back onto her lap. 'Just kidding. I won't mention your secret, don't panic.'

I look at her seriously. 'I'd rather you didn't talk to her, Rebecca. I think it would be better if you let me sort this out.' I can't believe how much I sound like a bad guy from a B-grade thriller.

CHAPTER SEVENTEEN

How close should you let your husband get to your mother? This question has plagued women since time immemorial. Should we even introduce our husbands to our mothers, or simply spirit them off to our bedrooms forever? Should we encourage them to bond?

I am of the spiriting away camp. There is nothing more offensive than seeing your husband helping your mother in the kitchen. The system of mother-in-law as daughter's confidante and bullier of husbands is a sacred feminist tradition. Seeing mothers bond with husbands is an affront to this revered custom. A betrayal of the mother – daughter relationship. How can a girl complain about her man to a mother who trusts him? Mothers who break this tradition should be lined up and shot.

Extract from a *New Yorker* article, 'Mother And Son-In-Law Bonding in the 80s' by Topsy Denier

Anna

A day has passed but I am still living my life waiting for the telephone to ring. I long to hear Mark's voice again. Going against all my earlier Andy Warhol principles about telephone relationships, I've now decided that I shouldn't place so much importance on the telephone.

I tell myself how old-fashioned this is. Telephones are so *over*. So definitively *un*. I should be hanging out in cyberspace where the action is, replying to e-mails from my fans. The truth, however, is that I haven't checked my e-mail since I sent the offensive letter to The Jerk. I am afraid of what his reaction might have been.

As soon as I sit at my keyboard, the phone rings.

I trip over my pile of soft toys, which take up a lot more room than they used to, thanks to the new additions Mark made to their number. I considered leaving them at his apartment, but I didn't feel it would be fair on the other toys. They'd bonded and

I didn't see why they should they be made to suffer just because things didn't work out between Mark and me.

I am terrified that it's him ringing to cancel as I say hello. But it is worse than that. 'Poor dear Mark,' Topsy sniffles on the other end.

'Who is this?' I ask (just to piss her off).

'I can't think what he has done,' she declares melodramatically. Topsy is always doing this. It is a very effective device but one which I suspect I could never carry off to any great effect.

'Why aren't you more supportive of my position in all of this? I *am* your daughter after all,' I remind her pathetically.

I have been reminding her that I am her daughter all my life, as if she is one of those coma victims that needs their past redefined for them.

She pretends to ignore me. 'All the poor boy wanted was a baby. How spiteful of you to punish him for wanting something that any sensitive, sweet man would want.'

'I'm not punishing him. I just felt like a failed baby machine,' I sigh, hoping for a bit of pity. 'I moved back here to get some perspective. We want different things, it's for the best. And I wish you would stop referring to him as "poor". He's not a bit poor. He's very rich, in fact. I'm the poor one in all this.'

'That's all I'm saying,' she sighs, but I very much doubt that it will be. 'I sense my opinion isn't welcome. Far be it from me to tell you how to live your life, Eggnog. You know I have never sought to do that.'

I'm not letting her off that easily. 'Well, how is he being punished then?' I demand.

It's hard to rattle my mother, though. 'Punished? You just told me you weren't punishing him. You told me you were looking for *perspective*.'

I feel the blood rush to my face. I am really angry now. 'If anyone's being punished it's me. Being made to feel guilty because I'm not pregnant. What is this, the Middle Ages?'

There is a pause during which I suspect she is conversing with someone else in the room.

'Are you with someone?' I ask.

'Well, if you must know, Mark stayed at the hotel with me last night.'

'Mark? Stayed with you? At the hotel? At The Pierre? You mean God-Boy?' I squeal, overwhelmed by the pain of it all. This is every daughter's nightmare and I say as much in a stream of badly constructed sentences and sobs.

'He doesn't actually like the term God-Boy, Eggnog. I know you mean it affectionately but he finds it patronising. He says it strips him of his individuality and reduces him to a masculine ideal he can never live up to.'

'Fuck off!' I yell down the phone line. 'If you want to get patronising here, what about him speaking to me through my own mother?'

Topsy makes sympathetic noises. 'He was very upset, Eggnog. Distraught. I could hardly send him off into the streets like that. Not at four am. Knowing how you feel about him, I didn't think you would want him to be alone at a time like this.'

I slam the phone down, and pull it out of the wall socket. I'm staggered that my own mother could betray me like this. She is a witch. An evil monster. A vision of Mark and her making out flashes across my synapses. I push it aside, but it remains tattooed on my consciousness. My worst fear realised. My mother stealing my lover. It feels very ancient Greek and wrong. I find a box of Captain Crunch and stuff my hand inside.

Sitting in a heap on the floor surrounded by my toys, I begin to cry. The toys look at me, distressed by my outpouring. I must try and pull myself together for their sake.

Maybe it has been going on for years, a voice of pathos within me suggests. *The Case Of The Disappearing Boyfriends Of Anna Denier*. It sounds worse than ancient Greek. It sounds like a CBS made-for-television thriller. Even though I doubt very much that it's true, I keep telling myself that it *could* be.

I stick on a Leonard Cohen CD, and when that doesn't work an old Smiths cassette, both given to me by my editor in London when we first got together. When he was still my mentor. The bathos of it all helps me to pull myself together. Peeling the cigarette from my lower lip, I shower and start building a strategy.

Mark has set our date for tomorrow night. I'll have to work fast to conceal the large spot that has appeared on my chin. It is at times like these that a girl needs a friend. And I don't mean a scatty friend who carries around the cursed slipper of a gangrenous guru. Last night she was trying to tell me that the depression about Mark wanting kids is due to the fact that I was a mother with nineteen kids in my past life. The soul of the man who sired this ginormous breed communicated this info to her on the astral plane. She's been going there a lot lately.

But I really *need* a friend now. Someone on a goodwill mission. Someone who wants to see me live happily ever after, someone with no links to the men of my past life. Rebecca is the only person who comes to mind. I brush aside her links to Mark by reminding myself that she is now engaged to Rob, an eminent gynaecologist – Vagina Man.

I plug the phone back in and dial her number. She answers on the first ring. It is as if she was waiting for my call, and this thought gives my ego a much-needed boost. After a brief exchange of girl talk we arrange to meet at Aubergine in half an hour. Aubergine is a café near me which serves a weird selection of Greek food with Manhattan overtones, stuff like eggplant, feta and olives on bagels.

'He's completely mad about you,' Rebecca mumbles through her eggplant bagel.

'So why is he so obsessed with using me as a womb?'

'He's not "obsessed". I don't think he's expressing himself well over this, that's all. Give him time. Every relationship has its problems,' she sighs. I notice dark circles under her eyes.

'Are you okay Bec, you look kind of tired.'

'It's nothing.'

'Crap. What is it?' I press.

'Well, Rob's been at me to sign a pre-nuptial promising not to burden him with kids for the first five years of our marriage.'

'You're kidding? And you're signing that?' I snort

in horror. My mild fondness for Vagina Man plummets.

'No, of course not. How dumb do you think I am? It was a sort of joke really, but that's not the point. I'm just saying he *wants* me to stay on the pill for five years.'

I can't help making a face.

'Don't make a face, I can see his point. As much as I would love a baby, it would be crazy to start a family now, just when we are both at the height of our careers.'

'Maybe you should tell Rob this stuff,' I suggest.

'No, Rob's right, this really isn't the time for starting a family. We should wait and see how the Millennium pans out.'

I point out that millenniums usually take a lot longer than most women's fertility cycles to pan out. She laughs. 'You know what I'm saying. Most men are afraid of children. The concept of getting up at night to change a diaper scares the hell out of them.'

The image of a shitty diaper makes me gag. Boy, does it not go well with my olives. 'It scares the hell out of me too!' I point out. 'Yuck!'

The waitress comes over and asks if we want anything else – just after Rebecca and I have stuffed oversized chunks of bagels into our mouths. It is like being at the dentist, caught between replying with our mouths full or grunting like Neanderthals. We shake our heads and laugh hysterically which scares the poor girl off.

'Do you think she was waiting for us to stuff our faces before she came over and asked?' Rebecca suggests when the girl is out of earshot.

'Definitely,' I say. 'All Manhattan waitresses are out to destroy all other attractive girls, and us specifically. Every last one of them is on a mission to undermine us at every opportunity.'

'And to flirt with our menfolk,' Rebecca adds.

'And it's very, very personal, too.'

We're giggling now and the staff don't look impressed by our mirth. 'Exactly! They're all trained up by ubersinister anti-girlfriends in New Jersey and then shipped in. Do you know, they even teach them to spit in our coffees?' I whisper covertly.

Rebecca smothers her laughter.

I can't hold myself back any longer – I like Rebecca. A lot. Real or not, she's just what I need at this point in time. After my third glass of wine I – perhaps inadvisably – admit that Rob is known to Mark and me as Vagina Man.

But she laughs so hard that the wine she's drinking

starts shooting out her nose. I guess you can never be too real for that. Rebecca is my kind of girl. So I tell her I named Mark God-Boy.

We spend the rest of the bottle renaming all the rest of Mark's friends. There is DBB (Death By Breath), Can-Head, Baboon-Bum and The UB (Ultimate Bitch), another one of Mark's girlfriends.

'You've got to give God-Boy a chance,' she tells me when we're saying our good-byes on the street. 'I mean Mark – I love that name God-Boy, it's so him. But seriously.'

'Please, not seriously. Don't say what I think you're going to say. Please.'

But she said it anyway. 'Give Mark another chance.'

I watch her as she does the button up on her grey Donna Karan coat and I am reminded once again of how chic she is.

'You guys are great together. Don't shoot yourself in the foot. Don't shoot him,' she pleads, holding my shoulder. 'I mean, it's not like he wants you to spank him with a slipper is it?'

'How did you know about that?' I ask, feeling the blush ride up my neck. 'It wasn't just any slipper, it was a very spiritual slipper, you know. Worn by a great guru—' I start, but she is laughing too hard. Besides which, he was very naughty,' I explain.

She laughs some more.

'Anyway, what about you? Promise me you'll talk to Rob about your desire for kids.'

'I'll think about it,' is all she'll say, but I know she won't. Out of the blue I ask something I've always wondered about. Now is my opportunity to dispel my whole jealous thing about her and Mark. 'Why didn't you and Mark, you know, make a go of it? You could have had a whole brood by now,' I probe, emboldened by the wine as I wrap myself up in my 70s vintage suede jacket.

'Mark? Mark and me?' she squawks in disbelief. 'We were only ever friends who slept together a few times after we'd both had too much to drink at college.'

'So what about the time on the kibbutz?'

I watch her as she reddens. 'The kibbutz?' she asks, as if she's never heard of it before. I nudge her in the ribs companionably. 'You and Mark went on a kibbutz one summer – don't tell me you don't remember. Mark mentioned something about it once. That must have been—'

But I am cut off when Rebecca spots a taxi heading towards us. She starts bouncing up and down, waving furiously. 'Oh look, there's a cab!' she cries out enthusiastically, as if she's never seen one before in her life.

Standing there in the light drizzle watching her drive away, I feel like she avoided my question intentionally. When the cab stops further up at the lights she turns around and waves merrily. But I feel uneasy now. I can't help it.

CHAPTER EIGHTEEN

I read your letter with some amusement. I especially liked the part where you used the bucket as a metaphor for the universal. This is exactly the kind of playfulness I'd like to see executed in your column. Perhaps you could include your views on your mother's suggestion that girls your age should put their eggs on ice in your next column? It's certainly a topical issue.
Keep up the good work.
Best wishes,
The Jerk

E-mail from The Jerk to Anna

Anna

I walk back home from my meeting with Rebecca via the ice-cream store on Bleecker, unable to shake a feeling that she had been concealing something to do with the reason she and Mark never got it together. Had something happened on the kibbutz that she didn't want to talk about? Rather than dispelling jealous fears by playing with the enemy, it seemed that I'd inflamed them.

When I come across a line outside the ice-cream store, I tag myself to the end and conjure up an idea of the flavour I'm craving. I'm so over cookie dough. In fact, I pledge never to have the cookie dough again. Even if it's the last flavour left in the world my lips will not part for cookie dough ice-cream. No way.

I check out my fellow ice-cream lovers. There is something reassuring about lining up that speaks to the one-time herd dweller within me, the all-night clubber, the girl who never leaves the dance floor – the girl, in short, who is no more.

Only the will to stand in line survives.

Maybe it's something I picked up from living in London that makes me unable to resist a pile up. I have to be part of it, and in the West Village this is no bad thing. I have met some of the coolest people in my pantheon of acquaintances while queuing in the West Village.

This night's no exception. There's a guy on the line selling firewood, who, upon noting the cigarette dangling from my lip, produces a lighter. How cool is that? I decline on the grounds that I'm trying to give up lighters but we get talking.

He's a sculptor, he tells me, as we rub our hands together for warmth and watch our breath mist up. He buys up the wood in mass, he explains, as he orders his chocolate chip ice-cream, then he sells on the bits that don't inspire him to cover his costs.

He's my age and – I notice as he takes a lick of his cone – kind of cute in a rumpled, hygiene-disinterested way. His name's Charles and I realise as I order wood that he is the sort of guy I might have considered prey before Mark. He promises to bring some wood round later that night and says good-bye.

After I pay for my ice-cream (okay, so I went for the cookie dough after all), I prop myself up at the bar so I can check out the activity on Bleecker. Everyone seems to be in couples – like those hunt dogs in

England. All of them rugged up in coats and scarves, laughing, arguing, cuddling, in the security that they are going to go home together and snuggle up. It is like Noah's Ark and I am like the animal left out alone to be taken by the flood waters of New York.

By the time I finish my ice-cream, a cold pit of loneliness has gathered in my heart. I pull my coat around my shoulders like some kind of Dickensian pauper, and trudge back to my flat as the first snowflakes of winter fall. To complete my misery the lift is broken again, so I climb the six floors up to my apartment, put on some music, sit at my computer and stare at my screen save – the dancing baby.

It is the last straw. All my doubts fall in on me then. I mean who am I kidding? Even Noah wasn't interested in girls who didn't want to breed. I ring Mark and leave a message on his machine cancelling our date.

Despite my conversation with Rebecca, or perhaps because of it, I know I can't just have one taste of Mark and walk away. I explain to the Upper East Side girl within that we have to be cruel to ourselves now, in order to be kind to ourselves in the future.

'Balls,' she swears. (It's a nasty turn of phrase she picked up from some of the pinched-looking women with small dogs in the lobby of Mark's apartment building.)

In time I will move through the pain barrier of my break-up. It seems implausible now, but life must go on. I plan to take massages and pedicures and change my hair colour, but I'm not that financially equipped, so I curl up with my toys, reading my mother's book instead, waiting for Charles to come with my wood.

Chapter ten and Topsy is discussing a court case that had taken place the year before in California, where a guy sued his ex-girlfriend for misuse of his sperm. The girl had conceived, despite having told him she was on the pill. He was seeking compensation for the trauma of having offspring he never wanted.

When the phone rings it's Topsy. 'I've been thinking, we should go shopping,' she decrees as soon as I pick up. I envisage her on the other end of the line, smoothing an errant hair back into place in her perfect French bun.

I also don't doubt that she is envisaging me, scrunched up like a piece of crumpled washing on my chair, wrapped up in my cardigan and a pair of woolly socks, my hair bunched into a scrunchy and my brow furrowed. Every fibre of my being screaming 'errant'.

'Why?'

'We need to do some building work on our relationship. My therapist told me that I need to work on my friendships.'

'Uh . . . I'm your daughter,' I point out. 'Our relationship was built in the womb. For better or worse, the job's been done, "Mom".'

'No need to be offensive,' she snaps.

I can tell my use of the word 'mom' has pissed her. 'Besides,' I point out. 'We've never shopped well together. You do Chanel, and my budget limits me to the Eighth Avenue flea market. We always argue, you always end up flouncing off, and I always end up crying.'

'But then we always go for one of our make-up lunches and that's the part I am really looking forward to, see.'

I acquiesce and agree to meet her in Barneys the next day. It will distract me from my broken date with Mark. That settled, I go back into file manager and pull up my latest column, a discussion of the etiquette of lining up to date in New York. Pretty soon I have a twitching muscle in my neck.

The buzzer goes just as I'm turning in for the night. I look at my watch. It's after midnight, but it's the wood guy and I buzz him up. The thought that he could be a serial killer, a rapist, a robber, crosses my mind, but like all women I ignore my survival instincts in favour of the not-making-a-guy-feel-like-I-don't-trust-him instinct.

Just the same, I fetch the hammer from under my sink to be on the safe side.

'My life partner's pregnant,' he announces as soon as I open the door.

'And?'

'That's why I'm late.' He pushes his way through and starts pulling in the bag of wood.

'Let me get this straight. You're late because your *life partner* is pregnant.' I am about to go into a tirade about how men blame all their faults on a woman's reproductive system. I've been reading too much of my mother's writing lately.

Charles holds up a hand in defence. 'No, she was about to give birth. At least we thought she was. We had to go to the emergency room. But as it was, it turned out to be Braxton Hicks.'

Whoops. I go bright red with shame. What kind of rad-fem harpy am I turning into? I'm becoming my mother, only minus the perfect hair, the immaculate nails, the sexy figure and the publicity agent.

I do an about face. Becoming incredibly sympathetic, I invite him to sit down and relax. I offer tea. 'So . . . Braxton thingamees. Wow! Is that like . . . really serious? Is everyone going to be alright?' I'm looking at him gently, like he's a cross between a fool and a senile woman lost on the streets of Manhattan.

I'm not actually that good at nurturing, really. I don't have the right features for it, or the right repertoire of facial expressions, the right tone even. I would make a lousy mom. My children would be intimidated by me.

Wood-man is disinclined to tarry anyway. He goes out and pulls in another bag of wood. 'Not serious, no. Just a pain in the butt. This lot should keep you going for a week.' He grabs a rag from the top of my computer and starts wiping his brow.

I look about the room, astonished by the amount of space a week's worth of wood takes up. I wonder how I'll fit in my apartment with all this wood. Then I realise that Charles's sweat rag is actually my one-time white Wonderbra, greyed after numerous washes in the wrong cycle.

I snatch it off him. Charles helps himself to a seat on top of Madeleine. 'It was good practice for the real thing though, see. Working out the time factor and that kind of stuff. It actually takes a lot longer to get to the hospital when you're in a hurry than you'd think. Of course, we went in the rush hour and the subway's always full and no one gives pregnant women a seat these days.'

I stare down at him in horror as I try to rescue Madeleine from under his butt. 'The subway? You raced your life partner to ER on the subway?'

Charles acts like I've just been telling him about the number of restaurants in the Village. He pulls Madeleine out, looks into her face for a bit and chucks her over to me. 'She looks like you,' he says. 'Cute.'

I snatch her back and stick her with the other toys.

'Do you have a kid?' he asks.

I blink, incredulous. 'Me? A mother? Are you kidding?'

'I just saw all the toys. Figured they must belong to someone.'

'They do. They belong to me.'

'Huh.'

'What do you mean "huh"?'

'No biggie.'

I clutch Madeleine tightly to my chest, my lower lip (cigarette attached) curled down.

He shrugs. 'Hit a nerve, hey? You've got issues, big deal, no need to be ashamed.'

'Ashamed?'

'Yeah, don't sweat it. I like a girl with issues, gives them fire. Anyway, where are you going to store all this wood?' he inquires, while I'm still thinking up a really great comeback to his dig about my toys and me having issues.

'I was thinking of here, as in the only room in the apartment sort of thing. Anyway, forget the wood.

Are you seriously telling me that you took your life partner to hospital on the train? What if she'd got felt up, or given birth even?'

He shrugs as he drags a bag of wood over to the small balcony. 'There's usually a doctor around, especially when it's busy. This will give you a bit more room. Do you want me to start a blaze for you?'

'You don't think that's a little . . . irresponsible?' I press.

'Irresponsible to light a fire with the wood you just had me lug round here? You buy the wood and now you don't want a fire? What kind of nut are you?'

'What kind of nut am I? I'm not the one dragging a heavily pregnant woman around the subway system as she's giving birth, buddy.'

I feel afraid all of a sudden as Charles stands up to his full height and comes toward me. 'She's used to the subway, we always use the subway. What's your problem, lady? Are you having that time of the month or something. You're acting really weird.'

'Lady? Lady? Huh!' I'd put the hammer down earlier on, around the time he started talking about his life partner expecting a baby. I guess he lulled me into a false state of security. But now I am going to show him how much of a lady I'm *not*. I start feeling around the back of the couch for the hammer.

Charles has his hands on his hips when I finally

recover my weapon. 'Pregnancy isn't an illness, you know,' he explains.

I produce the hammer and wave it around menacingly. 'Look, I'm the girl in this room, buddy. I'll tell you what pregnancy is and isn't. Okay?'

He stands up to me which I wasn't really expecting. If someone menaced me with a hammer, I'd probably just collapse at their feet and grovel pathetically. 'So how many times have you been pregnant then? How many kids have *you* got?' he sneers.

'I think you should go now,' I tell him, implying by the way I hold the hammer that not complying with my suggestion could easily end in homicide. His. 'How much do I owe you?'

He takes the hammer from me as easily as if it was candy from a baby and holds it behind his back. 'Forget the money. I want to settle this slur you've just made on my character.'

I make a few ineffectual grabs for the hammer and repeat my request for the bill. 'Tell me how much I owe you and you can go,' I say forcefully. Now that I've lost my weapon, I want this guy out of my life as quickly as possible. 'Who knows, maybe your wife's gone back into labour again.'

'Life partner. And I told you, she wasn't in labour. It was Braxton Hicks.'

'Which sounds even worse if you want my opinion.'

'Which I don't.'

I open the door and make an ushering movement. 'Listen, we could go on like this all night and still get nowhere. It's late, and even if your life partner doesn't need you, I want you out of my life.'

He nods wearily and shrugs his shoulders. He looks tired. He is big and gangly but somehow like a little boy. 'Alright then, just give me the money. Twenty bucks.'

We are interrupted when Sienna comes hurtling into the room at breakneck speed and starts flying through the air. For a second I think she's mastered a levitating spell, but as Charles and I scrape her off the floor she explains that she stumbled over the sack of wood. She isn't badly injured but Charles makes a huge fuss, insisting on carrying her over to the sofa and getting her a drink of water.

'Wow, talk about bad karma,' Sienna sighs as Charles fans her with a copy of *ID*.

'That's top quality hardwood you're talking about there,' he says, jumping to the defence of his wood.

'Not that. My crystal ball. It just revealed to me that I will fall in love with the next man to carry me.'

'Wow,' Charles exclaims.

I do this really false awkward laugh thing I picked up in London. 'Oh, didn't I introduce you? Sienna, this is Charles, he's got a life partner and she's having his baby.'

'Cool,' she enthuses.

'Yes, his life partner is having his baby. Any minute now I should think,' I add, giving Charles a v. stern look.

'Yeah, I'd better go,' he agrees, with an obvious degree of reluctance.

'I'll walk you down,' Sienna offers, and it isn't till they leave me alone that I realise I haven't paid Charles his twenty dollars.

CHAPTER NINETEEN

Formula feminism is outdated. The only thing that the disparate groups of feminists can agree on is that inequality based on gender is wrong and that it is up to individuals to choose the lifestyle they want. A woman's place is where she wants it to be. Be it homemaker or career woman, scone baking or boardroom management, it is a woman's duty to choose, and a man's duty to stand aside and let her make those choices.

Sexism isn't sexy.

Extract from *Don't Let Your Womb Hold You Back* by Topsy Denier

Anna

I am chatting away to Topsy at Barneys about Sienna's remarkable declaration of the night before. I mean, poor Charles, what had she been thinking? Topsy, as per usual, doesn't seem to be listening. She is leaning over, talking in a stage whisper to one of the counter assistants. 'She needs a light coverage, something to hide the shine of the T-zone region.'

Embarrassing? Uh-huh, you bet, and this is *nothing* for Topsy.

The counter girls pull at the skin around my eyes as if trying to dislodge my retina.

'So it's only the shiny T-zone she wants help with then?' one of the older matrons inquires of Topsy, as if I am not there at all.

'I am still here everyone,' I cry out. 'Even girls with shiny T-zones have feelings, you know!'

But to no avail.

'What about the sagging around the eye area and the lines around the mouth? Do you want me to prescribe something for that?' the matronly woman asks.

I go to open my mouth but Topsy interrupts. 'How nice of you to offer (reading the woman's name tag), Ms Thomas. Anything you can do to strip away those years, she'd be more than grateful. Wouldn't you, Eggnog?'

'Hang on,' I splutter. 'Not so much of the stripping back the years business, thank you very much, I'm only twenty-something, what are you trying to do? Turn me back into a foetus?'

'A girl can never be too young, whatever her age.' She pinches my cheek. 'Let Topsy spoil her little Eggnog, there's a good girl. And after the makeup lesson let me buy you a nice Prada. It's time you got rid of that knitted thing you persist in carrying around like it contains all your worldly goods. Let Topsy buy you something with a strong clasp and a good shine. You'll never be mugged with a shiny bag. Muggers are intimidated by shine, it's a fact.'

'Well then, my shiny T-zone should be enough to scare them off, shouldn't it?'

Topsy takes a sharp intake of breath. 'So defensive with your poor Topsy. I was just suggesting a new bag, Eggnog.'

I'm about to give a spirited defence of my bag, which wasn't knitted at all but was a genuine Victorian handbag I'd bought in London on the Portobello Road as a good-bye-to-England gift to myself, but

Topsy was already directing her attention back to the staff of the Chanel counter and shoving me into the makeup stool. 'Put her under the scrutiny of the lights. Let's expose every single flaw.'

'Oh yes, let's. Can we, please!' I squeal in mock delight, but my sarcasm falls on deaf ears as the girls thrust me into the dental-like chair and go to work, pulling, shoving, thrusting, brushing. It is like being trampled underfoot at the post-Christmas sales.

Just as I start spinning into unconsciousness, Topsy pats my arm in a strangely motherly fashion. 'Once we've got you looking *partially* presentable (as good as it ever gets with me in Topsy's book), we'll go and have a lovely lunch. You never know who you might meet at lunch.'

Her words should have made alarm bells ring, but my face is still covered in a flurry of brushes, liners and fingers. 'Just a little eyeliner,' Topsy instructs. 'And something to give her cheeks a little colour. You have been looking sallow, Anna.'

'It's called lack of sun, Topsy. And besides, you look like a porcelain doll. Your skin is so white you can see your veins.'

'I think you have beautiful skin, Ms Denier,' one of the girls simpers, poking a liner pencil up my nostril in the process.

'Yes, but unfortunately Anna didn't inherit *my*

complexion,' she sighs, as if the loss is still of great sorrow to her.

'That's right,' I confirm. 'I inherited the complexion of a man whose testicles belong in a liquidiser,' I tell the store at large, beating my mother to her chant.

'Don't all men's?' one of the girls giggles.

'Girls!' Topsy exclaims in her seductive drawl. No one can pronounce the word 'girls' like my mother. She can make it sound like an act of foreplay. 'Let's not be cruel. Everyone knows I *love* men,' she decrees, clasping her hands to her breasts. 'Anna's just walked out on a god of a man. A veritable icon of all that is good in his gender.'

'Well I think that's marvellous,' a short Chanel assistant agrees, giving my cheek a comforting pat. 'Good for you. Stand up for yourself. Even the good guys need to be treated roughly.'

I give my supporter a smile.

Topsy looks suddenly alarmed by the change of the tide. 'I disagree. If you find heaven, why go back down to hell?' she argues. I can't see her but I know that she is giving her hair the trademark stroke. She is saved from further dissent when a fan tugs on her sleeve and asks her if she is *the* Topsy Denier.

I hate the way my mother has a pronoun for a title.

Makeup and humiliation complete, we head onwards

and upwards to designer fashion, where Topsy insists on buying me the most gorgeous, tight-fitting Donna Karan dress.

I can't help myself. I love it and fawn. We haven't been shopping in years and I have forgotten how much fun she can be when her platinum credit cards are out. I almost feel like giving her a kiss of affection, especially when she forces me into a pair of breath-takingly high glass Sonya Rykiel platforms.

'See how the air is so much fresher up here?' Topsy enthuses as I clomp around the store. Catching sight of myself in the mirror, I do sense a cleaner, purer atmosphere, and a slimmer, slicker me. I look too good to be me, in fact. I look too damn fabulous.

Topsy and I giggle our way through the rest of the store like school girls stealing a day off from exam study. She presses a bag on me here, a jacket on me there, a scarf, a belt, etc., etc. And who am I kidding, I lap it up. This is the good side of Topsy and I'm not too proud to exploit it.

For all my problems with my mother, she is a phenomenon. Everyone stops her, everyone wants a piece of her, and Topsy, like the star she is, laps it up. Signing autographs, sharing advice, charming everyone. Yes, even me, up to a point. I'd be lying if I said I'm not proud. My mother is single-handedly responsible for glamorising a woman's right to choose.

Before my mother, anything to do with women's rights smacked of lesbianism, hairy arm-pits and masculinity. She was the first feminist to coin the phrase, 'Sexism just isn't sexy'.

When my mother burnt her bra in 1983 (a publicity stunt for one of her books), men fell and wept amongst the ashes. 'Don't worry, it wasn't a good one,' she reassured viewers on a talk show later that week, as if she was trying to stop rioting in the streets.

She's made the choices that men have always enjoyed seem a possibility for women. But she is an individualist first and foremost, an original. Somehow this feminist in siren's clothing has struck a chord from America's trailer parks to Fifth Avenue.

All my life I have been jealous of her achievements, telling myself that her success has interfered with her loving and nurturing of me. Telling myself that her political agenda with men has prohibited my relationship with my father.

She puts her hand through mine as we walk down the street to the restaurant. I notice that passers-by smile at us as we swing our shopping bags in the air to hail a cab. I guess that as a girl I've always respected her, but as her daughter I feel that Topsy Denier suiting herself, hasn't always suited me.

I start to warm to her as she points out shops and

people on the drive uptown. Distracted with my spirit of reconciliation, I don't ask where it is we're going. So naturally I'm caught off guard to discover Mark waiting for us at the restaurant.

I walked right into that one, I guess.

CHAPTER TWENTY

Exes are people you once seduced. People you convinced for a moment of your sophistication, your wiles, but who now know what you look like in your B-grade underwear.

The scary thing about bumping into exes is that they have information about you that could be dangerous if it fell into the wrong hands. That's why couples stay together because they don't want this information out there where it could hurt them.

Extract from the 'New York Girl' column of Anna Denier

Dear Anna,
See what you can do to fluff this piece up a bit. We are trying be more touchy-feely in the new century – new start and all that? Know you'll manage something.
Best wishes,
The Jerk

Anna

He looks amazing. Even in my heels, I notice that he's taller than me. Even in his suit, I can see the contours of his body. He is Zeus disguised as a swan. I am a mere mortal – a Leda. Now I see him for what he really is and I see the danger. He is a god who wants to continue his line and needs a mortal with whom to do it. Whereas I am content to see my own line die out if it means I don't have to push a buggy around the streets of Manhattan and warm baby food in my kitchen.

He sweeps me up into his arms and tells me I smell wonderful. I feel light as a feather, giggly, delicious. But the words that come out of my mouth suggest none of this adoring love-struckness.

'How dare you,' I begin, glaring at Topsy. It's a principle thing again – my principles are always getting me into trouble. I feel like slapping her. 'You!' I point at her. 'How could you?'

She smiles awkwardly, flustered. Looks down at her Cartier watch and jerks at the shock. 'Oh my, is that the time? I have a television appearance in five seconds. Sorry to eat and run darlings. We'll do it again, shall we? Soon! Ciao.' She pinches my cheek and practically smooches Mark.

'You haven't eaten!' I call out to her as her heels click-clack up the street towards Madison. 'This is a straight case of hit and run,' I yell at her disappearing form.

'I think she was trying to help,' Mark offers awkwardly as pedestrians stare at me and she disappears into a cab. Despite being Zeus, a god from the heights of Olympus, I sense he is out of his depth here outside Le Cirque on East 65th Street.

'Meeting you here. It was her idea. I told her you'd be pissed. But Topsy isn't really the sort of woman you argue with,' he explains, with a wry smile fidgeting about his lips.

I'm not sure I really like the way he is blaming Topsy. I mean, she is a bitch, granted, but he could at least act the gentleman and take the rap. I turn on him. 'And I *am* the sort of woman you argue with? Is that what you're trying to say? I'm the sort of woman best barefoot and pregnant in my place on the mantelpiece. Along with all the other trophies of your manhood.'

He looks stuck for a retort, hands in pockets and head bowed. I don't know how I come up with these things so quickly, really I don't. I should be listed as a dangerous weapon and never given a licence to use myself.

But he looks up at me sheepishly and laughs, his fantastic laugh, the one that makes me aware of how much I love him. 'So you're not hungry, I take it?'

What's a girl to do? My heart takes over from my brain. I submit and ask him to lead on.

'How's Sienna?' he inquires, dipping his bread in the saucer of olive oil.

'She's worrying me actually. I think she fancies my wood guy.'

'So?' he says blandly, sticking the bread in his mouth. He even looks good when he chews.

'He's in a relationship,' I remind him. 'His life partner's about to have a baby!' I pause so that the magnitude of this can sink in.

'Bummer.'

'She's always falling for the wrong guy.' I shake my head, as if this is a disease with which I am not afflicted myself, and suck my oysters from their shells suggestively. I'd knocked back two Manhattans as soon as we were seated so I was feeling relaxed and flirty but totally unprepared for what came next.

'I want to be with you Anna.' His hand reaches out to touch my face.

All my tensions return.

'We're so great together.' He takes hold of a strand of my hair while staring into my eyes earnestly. 'I love you no matter what.'

I nod.

'I mean it, Anna,' he says, taking my hand.

'You want kids Mark. You think I'll change my mind one day, but what if I don't?'

He frowns, plays with the swizzle stick in his soda. 'This isn't just about kids.'

My next dozen oysters arrive. I start sucking them down straight from the shell like Mark had shown me.

'Why do we have to think about kids now? We've haven't even been together for a year yet,' he argues.

I brush this detail aside. 'You can't say this *isn't* about kids. That's exactly what it's about. You forget, I saw how you were gutted over the false alarm. You want kids, you can't lie.'

He mutters something but I don't hear it and I don't wait for him to repeat it. 'Face it, Mark, we are two people who want different things. You want a wife, a family, career fulfilment, savings plans and dinner parties.'

He looks at me like I'm a complete stranger. 'I want you, Anna,' he says simply.

I want to believe that it's that simple but it's pointless. The truth is destiny, as Sienna is always saying.

He takes one of the thousand AWOL hairs of my head and puts it back in its scrunchy – the last vestige of Anna Denier the slob. 'I want you, Anna Denier. From the cigarette on your lip to your cat's ears, to your crazy way of keeping house. I don't want you to change one hair of this chaotic head. Can't we just go back to the way we were?'

'Wasn't that a film?' I ask, evading his gaze. '*The Way We Were*? I think it was. Barbra and Robert, wasn't it?'

He runs the side of his hand down my face and I feel a surge of electricity go through me. I want to do anything and everything he says. His eyes are reaching into my being, searching for that free radical I-want-a-baby cell.

'You're totally hedging the issue of kids,' I point out. 'I saw your face when I told you I might be pregnant. Like all guys, you're looking for a vessel to propagate your seed. An ovum to impregnate.' As I'm giving this little speech, all I really want to do is throw myself into his arms.

'Let me say something—'

'Mark—'

'Anna, this is getting out of hand. I have to tell you something. Something I should have told you when things first started to get serious between us.'

'You're secretly harbouring a wife and kids already?'

I joke, but he doesn't even look at me. He's nursing his head in his hands.

'I was only joking,' I tell him.

'Oh fuck, this is a mess. I wish . . . I should have told you ages ago.'

'Told me what?'

'There never seemed to be the right time, and then you thought you were pregnant and then it was too late to tell you. It happened when—'

He's distracted as the waiter comes over with his main course. Seared swordfish in tarragon sauce.

'Let me save you the trouble,' I start, before he can continue.

'Here's my half of the bill,' I say, placing some cash onto the table. 'I think we're just kidding ourselves if we go on.' Pulling the last note from my new purse, I know that I will have to take the subway home but I don't care. I'm so wrapped up in misery I could travel home on a refugee convoy and not care.

In fact, by the time I have transplanted myself back to Hudson, I feel like a refugee – a refugee of my own heart. My brain is frozen on the image of him sitting there in the restaurant, telling me of his plans for our future.

Despite all my rational justifications for saying and doing what I did, despite the fact that I know I'm right, I want nothing more than to feel his arms around me.

How did things ever get this complicated?

CHAPTER TWENTY-ONE

Even single girls fall in love. It's nothing to be ashamed of. I fell in love this summer, only I kept it from you to save you the hurt and misery that ultimately follows Falling In Love. Don't get too excited, he wasn't a real man or a genuine contender for long term commitment, more a God-Boy really. He was rich, nipple-curlingly gorgeous and funny – like I said, he wasn't real. Put it this way, if I'd tried to photograph him, he would have vaporised in the viewfinder.

Extract from the 'New York Girl' column of Anna Denier

Anna

It is two weeks since my disastrous lunch with Mark
and I am still licking my wounds. I've hardly been out,
except for fags. I've started rolling my own while I lie
in front of the feeble flames of my fire. It feels kind of
rustic. Girl of the elements, etc.

Charles never did come back for his money, and my
wood stocks have all but run out just as I've started to
depend on the fireplace for company. John Lennon
once said that the television is the twentieth-century
fireplace but I've never been good at television. For
one, I'm worried that Topsy will be on every channel
chatting about a 'woman's right to have it all and
then some'. The other thing is how remote the remote
always seems – I'm always losing it down the back of
the couch or in the bed covers.

I am rationing my wood stocks now as if the end
of the world has come and this is the only source of
fuel in the city. I imagine scenes of chaos and violence
on the streets of Manhattan, and then I realise that it's
not my imagination – there really *are* scenes of chaos

and violence on the streets out there. It's only in my apartment that things are so dull.

Tomorrow night will be Halloween, and as a precaution I've stocked up on chocolate for the trick-or-treaters, but now of course I've eaten most of it. I've started eating chocolate chips with milk as a cereal and Orky bars as nutritious snacks. There'll be nothing left tomorrow at this rate and I'm expecting to be lynched.

I envisage what it would be like if I had a child, trying on its scary outfit now in anticipation. I imagine myself hustling children out the door of my Upper East Side apartment for up-market trick-or-treating.

Could I be up for that?

As much as I want the answer to be yes, it remains stubbornly, no. The fire throws shadows about the room. I think of my prospective daughter as a witch, my future son as a sorcerer. I think of myself dressed to match as high priestess or sugar plum fairy and I begin to sink – how depressing. The intercom buzzes but I don't get up; I don't want to see anyone.

I add one of the last five logs to the blaze. Perhaps the fact that I can imagine myself with children at all is something in itself.

I go over to the full-length mirror and puff my tummy out as far as it can go. I look about three months gone. Mark has always revelled in my flat tummy and my pert breasts, such as they are. I run my hands down them. Actually, they're not that pert, just flat, basically. Flatter than my tummy. Almost concave, really. The buzzer goes again and I answer it as an alternative to facing my chest.

It's Charles come for his money. I buzz him up then hurriedly throw some clothes on, and have only just unearthed the hammer when he enters with a small pouch on his chest.

'I've come for the twenty dollars,' he announces sullenly as he enters. The lump on his chest begins to mew. I look into the lump where a tiny baby is squirming.

'Wow!' I say. 'She had it then?'

He smiles. 'After I saw you, I got home and she said "This is it!" I didn't believe her at first. Not after the Braxton Hicks episode.'

I nod, remembering the slide show of that night.

The pouch makes another little squawking sound. 'She's cute,' I offer, staring into the amazing newness of the life squirming against his chest. A tiny mouth groping vainly for a nipple. Something inside me goes whoosh. An oestrogen rush?

'After what you said about the subway and all, I took her to hospital in a taxi. I guess I should thank you for that.'

'Forget about it.'

'Nah. I was being a jerk. You were totally right. She gave birth on the gurney as they wheeled her in. Knocked me out seeing her diving out of her mother like that. We called her Leda.' He kissed her head proudly.

'Leda? As in Leda and the swan?' I ask.

'You don't think it's too pretentious do you?'

'No, it's a great name.'

He seems stupidly relieved. 'Thanks. She flew out like a cork, man. I couldn't believe it. It's like, I wasn't really expecting a "baby". Not a fully formed one at least.'

The question begged – what was he expecting? Running his finger lovingly down Leda's cheek, he looks up and smiles at me. I smile back.

'She's so cute,' I repeat, at a loss before such tiny perfection. I can smell her head, like sugar and spice and all things nice in the world. 'Wow,' I say.

He laughs. 'Yeah. Wow is right. You can't believe it till it happens to you, man. It's amazing. I mean, it's like you have nine months to prepare, but nothing really prepares you for this. Look at her.'

I look.

'She's like a real person,' he points out.

'She is, isn't she?' I agree, looking at her virtually transparent eyelids flickering.

'A real living being. And she's mine, I mean ours.'
He shakes his head 'I can't get over her, man.'

I give him a goofy smile and stroke Leda's head.
'She's amazing,' I agree. 'Awesome, ubercool.' I wow
and coo with Charles. Maybe wanting children *is*
infectious. Maybe I'll catch something if I stick close
enough to him.

'And she never makes a noise, you know. Like you
think, oh boy, a kid. It's going to be loud, right?'

I nod energetically. That's exactly what I do think.

'But no. She's like, so quiet. I just stare at her all
night and count her breaths.'

I realise then that I have been counting Leda's
breaths, too. Her tiny eyelids are closed and her
cheeks puffed out. Her little bow-shaped mouth is
pursed. She is sucking as if there was a nipple in her
mouth or something.

I'm still holding the twenty dollars out to Charles
but I want to offer him more. Would it be rude
to offer a hundred dollars to hold his little girl. A
thousand, just to let me inhale her head for a night.
He takes the twenty and shoves it carelessly into his
jeans pocket.

'Everything changes, man. Everything. Before, I
really wanted to go out with the guys all the time,
or hang out in my studio listening to music and
drinking beers. Just, you know, looking at wood

and wondering what I can see in it. Now I'm like, no, fuck, leave me alone. I've got Leda. I don't want anything or anyone else.'

'What about your wife?' I ask.

'My significant other? Klarissa you mean? Yeah, well, she still wants all that stuff. She's not as into Leda as me. But man, I've got it bad. I am gone on Leda so bad it's insane. Klarissa's breast-feeding and all that but to her it's a chore. And I'm there wishing I could breast-feed. I'm there wishing I could do it all. 'Rissa thinks I'm mad, man. She was the one who wanted kids, too. I just went along with it. I never thought it would be like this.'

'Can I hold her?' I ask, emboldened by my own need.

He looks at me for a while as if sizing me up and I realise that I'm still holding the hammer. Whoops. I put it down on a counter awkwardly. Charles looks at the hammer and looks at me.

'Um . . . I was worried. Nothing personal,' I blurt, knowing how lame I sound. Is there anything more personal than a mad woman with an unlit roll-up cigarette stuck to her lip, wielding a hammer at you and your daughter?

But he doesn't appear to be listening. He is carefully prizing his pride and joy out of the papoose. I feel like I am growing, turning into a giant, like

Alice in Wonderland, as he passes her over. It's like passing a divine test when she doesn't cry as I hold her. I am looking for significance, signs from God. Portents. And this is definitely portentous.

'She likes to be held like this,' he demonstrates, just as Leda's head falls onto her toes.

'Does she have bones yet?' I ask, struggling to hold her as he's shown me.

'Yeah, course she does. They have all that stuff when they're born. Just no muscles.'

'Hey, like astronauts?'

We laugh. Leda is unbelievably light. And gorgeous. She's got skin that would make Isabella Rossellini green with envy. I hold her to my heart and inhale her head. 'How do babies get to smell like this?' I ask.

He chuckles. 'Isn't it wild? Fuck drugs. I mean, I can get high just sniffing the line of her eyebrows! Check them out, aren't they cool?'

I sniff one of her eyebrows and feel the rush. We are looking at one another and laughing. I can actually see why people have these kid things. I offer tea, but Charles has to go. Leda likes to feed at hourly intervals, he explains.

I thrust her back in his arms. Appalled. 'Hourly?'

'You got it. Pretty brutal on the sleeping this parenting.'

'Wow. That's harsh,' I say. 'Even in the night?'

'Round the clock. My little girl likes her mom and dad to get busy! Don't you Leda?' he asks, holding his daughter above him. She goes right on sucking, oblivious to her station in life. Up or down, she requires round the clock sucking.

Charles looks completely exhausted now that I scrutinise him. Like someone is sucking the life out of him from within. Then I realise that the someone is a seven-pound dumpling called Leda.

I go over to my toys and grab Miss Piggy. 'Maybe Leda would like this?' I suggest.

Charles accepts Miss Piggy. 'Are you sure?'

I try to sound light and jokey but my voice catches. 'I'm sure. Miss Piggy, my mentor of mentors since I was five years old must go where she is needed.'

He looks at me knowingly. 'Thanks, Leda will appreciate that.'

'Sure.'

'Do you want more wood?' he asks as I am opening the door.

'Yeah, actually I do. Can you bring it soon?'

'I'll just turn up,' he says.

'What if I'm not here?'

'I'll sell it to one of my other contacts.'

'I'm a contact? I've never been a contact before.'

'Well you're in the loop now!' he says, high-fiving

me as he goes. I hear voices on the stairs after I shut the door. Sienna's raucous laughter echoes upwards.

I go back to the toys and hug Madeleine to me and comfort her about the loss of Miss Piggy. Besides, I've held a baby. An actual baby. Miss Piggy is gone but I'll get over it. Hey, I'm in the loop.

CHAPTER TWENTY-TWO

Dear Anna,
I have been reading your column avidly since you returned to
New York and I love it. My only criticism is your treatment
of God-Boy. I mean, if he's so great, what's the biggie?
Signed,
Single and jealous as hell. New Jersey

Dear Anna,
Get – a – problem – girlfriend! This God-Boy sounds like
heaven on a stick. If you lose him, you'll deserve to die alone
in your flat and be eaten by rats.
Respectfully,
Carol. Brooklyn

Dear Anna,
I am a forty-nine-year-old spinster and already losing my
hair. Judging from the photograph above your column, you
are still offensively young and cute. I'd just like to point
out that one day you might be pushing fifty and bald and
you might regret your decision to cut this God-Boy guy out
of your life.
All the best,
Demoralised. Upper West Side

Anna

I spend Thanksgiving working my ovaries off to try and appease The Jerk with a knock-your-single-girls'-socks-off column that will back the hearts of my readers and convince them of my commitment to the single-girl life.

It isn't as if I have ever been very good at Thanksgiving, anyway. No practice, I guess. We never celebrated it in my family, owing to a lot of deeply mysterious political points that I found confusing as a child. In Topsy's view, holidays represent all that is bad in a patriarchal society. In her view they exclude women and celebrate men.

'We must *never* give thanks to anything that celebrates male hegemony,' she decreed gravely when I asked why we had no feast days in our family – with the notable exception of Easter which we celebrated simply as Egg Day. Actually, we didn't celebrate very much at all, the virgin birth being a particular sore point with Topsy.

So here I am in sweats, topped off with a woolly

hat and a pair of Mark's socks I'd kept for sentimental reasons. My column has been getting negative feedback since my public declaration about not wanting to be a womb for any man. There has been a lot of reader e-mail lately of the 'Dear Anna, are you insane? Snap up this God-Boy post-haste!' variety.

The Jerk informs me of his irritation at the disillusionment of my fans via e-mail. He suggests that I get my private life sorted out. 'In order' is the term he uses.

'Are you seriously telling me that my loyal, single flirty-something readers want me to become a turncoat to their cause and marry?' I screech down the cyber pathways.

'Yes,' he replies.

I am devastated that I have got it so wrong. My perception of New York as a throbbing, fast-paced city, brimming with café society, bars, clubs, sirens, is disintegrating. In reality, it is a city in therapy for loneliness. A city full of girls who don't really want to be single at all, who closely follow The Rules in the hope of nabbing a man who doesn't mutter to himself too much?

New York is full of girls who view my chucking of Mark as, well ... uberperverse. My loyal readers think I am brainless, clueless and cold-hearted for not nailing him to the floorboards of his apartment and ringing up a celebrant.

'Maybe Topsy paid them?' Sienna suggests idly when I seek her advice on my turncoat readers.

'Anything is possible with Topsy,' I have to concede.

Even The Jerk is suggesting that I do the right thing and marry him. 'Think of the ratings,' he pleads.

'This isn't television,' I point out, but he doesn't care about such details. Readers, ratings, revenue, whatever. The Jerk didn't get where he is today bothering about facts.

So now I am sitting at my computer watching my wretched dancing baby screen save and dwelling on the advice pouring in from my readers. There are thousands of unopened e-mails on my computer, but it is becoming clear that they all say pretty much the same thing – 'marry the guy'.

'What you need,' The Jerk tells me, 'is a good man who knows the meaning of romance.'

I hold back on sending my metaphorically playful reply, and stick to the simple but no less eloquent, 'FUCK OFF!'

Sometimes less is more.

In an act of sheer desperation I do what any girl feeling sorry for herself would do as an alternative to sticking her head in the gas oven. I have a radical (and ubertragic) hairstyle change.

'Do something drastic!' I demand, swooping into Robert Kree's salon on Bleecker Street. To be fair, they all try to talk me out of it – especially on the colour issue.

'Aubergine? Are you sure you want hair the colour of a vegetable that's so last year?' they argue. But what the staff and customers of Robert Kree fail to recognise is that I am on a mission to turn my life around. And a new hairdo is the most effective way to do just that, as women discovered back in the Ice Age.

And boy does my life need turning. If I'm honest, I am also kind of seduced by the idea of becoming unrecognisable, and if it means looking like last year's vegetable, so be it. Like I said, drastic is the key word.

The phone is ringing when I get back to my apartment, and I am relieved to hear Rebecca's voice. I tell her about my hair change. She'd seen Topsy on *Regis and Kathy* that morning and understands precisely where I am at.

'You poor thing,' she sympathises. 'I mean, I agree with what everyone's saying, but to have your private relationship debated on breakfast television must be *so* weird.'

'It is weird,' I tell her . 'But no weirder than having your first period studied at Berkeley.'

'Actually, that wasn't why I rang,' she interjects. 'I called to ask you out to lunch. The thing is, I need to talk to you.'

'Only if you promise not to mention marriage,' I agree, suddenly catching sight of my reflection in the mirror. I look like the meal I had eaten at my farewell dinner in London.

'But that's all I talk about these days. You might even call it an obsession. It's kind of a traditional topic for brides to discuss, funnily enough,' she points out sarcastically. 'You may not want my advice, but I need yours.'

'Fair enough,' I agree as I shake my new curls in the mirror. Rebecca explains that she's having a day off.

'I've been feeling really queasy,' she explains. 'Not sick exactly, just a bit, dunno, a bit off. Pre-marriage nerves, according to Vagina Man.'

'How is Rob?' I ask, scooping my hair up and piling it on top of my head. All I need now is a tiara, a ball and a carriage. Visions of me sweeping around the Avenues of NY in one of those horse-drawn carriages that lurk along the edges of Central Park suddenly seems seductive.

'He's fine, same, same. You know, I think he's even more excited than me about the wedding. Of course, his latest obsession is the stag night.'

'Groan, groan and double groan,' I declare. Stag nights are the ultimate Boy Zone.

'Yeah, I agree. He's viewing it as a kind of professional networking exercise, I think. Most of the guests he wants invited are the husbands of women he's treating. It seems like New York is a hot-bed of women with fertility problems, desperate to put their wombs and their check accounts in my fiancé's name. I don't know whether to be flattered or jealous.'

'It's your wedding too,' I remind her. 'You *are* going to have a send off as well. You have to promise me you're going to get disgustingly drunk on your hen night and embarrass yourself for your friends' amusement. I would find it a moment of personal satisfaction to see you dance on a table. I'm sure most of your friends feel the same.'

'Well, that was why I wanted to see you today. Well, that and the scoop.'

'The scoop?'

'Get this. Rob's agreed to let you and me arrange *his* stag night!'

I wait a beat. 'Is he insane? Does he know how much damage two girls who refer to him as Vagina Man can do to him and his clients over the course of an evening?'

'No, wait, let me finish. He's going to sort my hen night with his friends.'

'By "sort" you mean exactly – what? Turn it into a Tupperware party?'

'No, it's going to be great, Anna. We've made a solemn oath to one another to go completely overboard. He's going to create my fantasy hen night and I'm going to create his fantasy stag night.'

I am as intrigued as I am dubious. It sort of smacks of a sicko sex game that could easily go wrong. I have no idea what Vagina Man's fantasy stag night might involve, but given the way he spends his days looking up women's orifices, it is probably pretty unsavoury.

'I sort of thought you might advise me?'

As gratified as I am to know that someone still wants my advice, I can't help feeling suspicious. 'Um . . . let me get this clear. He'll arrange your hen night and you'll arrange his stag night?'

'Yeah.'

'And you're absolutely certain he isn't going to throw you a Tupperware party?'

'No way.'

'Gosh, well, I guess—'

'I want to go completely OTT, Anna. I mean it. That's why I want your help.'

'I don't know whether to be insulted or flattered.'

'I want this to be a night that *no one* forgets,' she insists, and I can tell by the quaver in her voice that she is on the edge of squealing. 'I've got this idea, see. I think we should hire three adjacent suites at the Paramount, and hold the stag night in one suite, the hen night in another, with the suite in the middle acting as a sort of green room where we can all meet up, make out, etc. I think it could be totally cool.'

'I'm still not getting it,' I tell her. 'Won't he just hire some lame cabaret act?'

'Sceptic.'

'And PS, are you really intending to hire strippers for your own fiancé?'

'Better than strippers. I'm getting in this *gatoy* troupe.'

'*Gatoy* troupes being . . . ?'

'Lady-boys. They're this famous group from Thailand I read about. *So* gorgeous, and seriously sexy.'

'Lady-boys?'

'They're boys who've had, well, become girls, only they're more girly than real girls,' she giggles. 'But they really are drop-dead gorgeous,' she assures me. 'And so talented.'

My mind actually boggles. I'm serious. I know, boggle is one of those experiences that our generation doesn't think it will ever have. Especially Village Girls. Mind boggling is more or less something I have made it my life's work to do to others. So to experience it first hand is kind of cool in a way.

'Ouch. You don't think Vagina Man will drop dead when he finds out? And what about his clients' husbands?'

'That's just it. He expects me to do something lame, that's why I'm upping the anti. These guys are *very* professional.'

'Yeah, well, we sure as hell don't want your intended running around with a bunch of *amateur* lady-boys, do we?'

'Come on, Anna, I thought you'd be into this.'

'I am,' I promise, not wanting to spoil her Big Night with my jaded cynicism. Besides, though not entirely convinced by her arguments, I'm intrigued. 'So the green room concept, let me get this straight. Anyone can go into the green room?'

'Uhuh.'

'Even the *gatoys*?'

'The green room is open but only guys can go into the stag room and only girls can go into the hen room.'

'So are the *gatoys* girls or boys?'

'Both.'

'The mind boggles again,' I laugh.

'But you think it's a good idea, though?' she presses.

It takes me a while to answer. Deep down, I'm a little worried. It all sounds too much like my serialised dream. The one where the all-male party rages in the next room, while I languish bored and listless in the room next door watching *I Love Lucy*.

'Well?'

'It sounds great in principle, as long as you're certain that we're not going to be stuck in a room full of girls with a Tupperware demonstrator burping plastic containers, while the guys are in the next room going hell for leather with the lady-boys. You have to promise we're talking strippers and hard drugs and not canapés and seventies records.'

'Anna, have no fear. We are going to push the boat out on this one. And when I say push it out, I mean all the way. We are sticking a motor on the back of this party and taking it out to the deep sea of the hen night experience. We are going to make Ernest Hemingway wish he had been born a girl.'

'Well, as long as you're providing life jackets.'

'Besides, he knows if he screws this up, I'll never forgive him. And let's not forget he's going to be stuck with me afterwards, for better or worse, sickness or health.'

'So you're sure the *gatoys* aren't going to be a sore point? I mean, you're stuck with Rob for the rest of your marriage too,' I remind her.

'That's why I wanted to meet up with you. Let's do lunch at Saks and I'll go through it with you. I need to pick up some concealer, anyway. I've developed these dark rings around my eyes.'

I catch my reflection in the mirror, shake my head and watch the curls dance. 'Okay, I'll see you at one. Give my love to Vagina Man.'

'Will do, and by the way, he wanted me to tell you that you should move back in with Mark. According to him, you are just what Mark needs. There, that's off my chest,' she breezes.

'Off your chest and into my face, gee, thanks.'

'He thinks you are just what Mark needs,' she repeats.

Actually, I didn't want to be what Mark, or any man for that matter, needed. 'It makes me sound like a service provider. I want the man of my dreams to *want* me, to *dream* of me, *desire* me, not *need* me. The moment I become useful, I know I'm doomed.'

'Just get it together, Anna,' she says simply.

CHAPTER TWENTY-THREE

To mother: means to nurture, to rear, to care for, to feed, to protect. To father: means to sire, to impregnate, to shoot your load.

A guy can perform his part of the parental bargain when he's drunk.

A woman has to devote her life to her role.

Today, thanks to technological advances enabling human egg retrieval and donation, we can throw off these falsehoods. We can enjoy the same freedoms as men, namely to be the biological parents of offspring we never have to see. We don't even have to give birth anymore.

So why is it that everywhere we look governments are limiting women's access to these technologies under the guise of foetal rights? Get your conscience out of our wombs!

Extract from *I'll Have Mine On The Rocks!* by Topsy Denier

Anna

I see Rebecca first. She looks like a lost child, standing amongst the Stilla product counter. Apart from a general bedraggled aura about her, she's lost weight in the weeks since our last rendezvous in the West Village. All of it off her face.

She is applying her lipstick, oblivious to my arrival. Her hair looks like it needs a trip to the salon, too. It resembles Ivana Trump's on a really windy day. She must be in a v. bad place to let herself go like this.

Out of place in my seventies suede jacket thing and my favourite knee-high lace up boots, I can feel other shoppers' eyes stalking me through the store. This is my first outing as an aubergine.

As she spots me and waves, I can't help focusing on the fact that I'd only seen Mark once since I'd last seen her, whereas she sees him most days. I feel a momentary twinge of jealousy, but then seeing how pale she looks, how exhausted, I force myself not to go to that place. I can't afford the return fare.

We make the obligatory kissing sounds in the

direction of one another's cheeks. I tell her she looks well. She tells me not to lie. Then, to press the honesty point home, she asks me why my hair looks like an eggplant.

'It's not eggplant,' I snap. 'It's aubergine.'

'Oh, as in the restaurant? Is that what gave you the idea? The eggplant on your bagel? Oh my God!' she cries, slamming a hand to her mouth.

'No it wasn't,' I reply stiffly. 'I didn't even have an eggplant bagel, I had feta and olives.'

She can see I'm peeved and softens. 'I'm not being mean, I've just never seen anyone with eggplant hair before, but you know what? I love it.' She smiles warmly and takes me by the hand. 'You look really cute. And I love the curls. I can see it's done marvels for the condition of the hair shafts.'

I try and jolly up as we wander around the makeup counters, trying on a lipstick here, a perfume there, an eyeliner, a mascara, and anything else running a tester, basically.

'So what have you been up to? How's the column going?' she asks at Clinique. We're trying out moisturiser. If you buy two products you get a tote bag and the most useless coloured lipstick known to girlkind.

'Alright,' I sigh, saying a firm no to an overly helpful assistant who swears she has just the thing to close my pores.

Rebecca squirts me with a perfume tester at Givenchy. I squirt her back. We are only halfway round the store but we are already starting to smell like a chemical factory. 'You're missing him Anna, face it.'

'What?' I yelp in pain as she sprays me again. This time my eye has taken a direct hit.

'Look at yourself, your face says it all. Not to mention the eggplant disaster.'

My eye is stinging like mad. 'You said you liked it,' I challenge, dabbing at my injured eye with a tissue I've already used to take off my lipstick.

She gives me a cuddle, apologising for being a bitch. Only she immediately negates the apology by saying she was just being honest.

PS: Being honest leads to nuclear arsenals being unleashed.

'He's really gutted, Anna. He's in a state. He doesn't want to use you as a womb, you've got that all wrong. Whatever else he's done, he's never wanted that.'

One word stands out from the puzzle. 'What do you mean by that? What else *has* he done?'

Rebecca starts to say something but a shop assistant comes over to offer help. I ask for more tissues. When she leaves, I press the point. 'Come on, what gives? What did you mean before about "whatever else he's done"? What else *has* he done? I want to know!'

She looks guilty. 'Look, it's none of my business. You're right, let's avoid talking about Mark today.' She's wearing a painful-looking grin and, feeling sorry for her, I agree to relent. I take the tissues from the kind attendant and clean myself up in the mirror.

'Okay, deal,' I agree. 'Let's talk about why *you* look like such crap,' I joke, but her response is to grab me as if she's about to make a citizen's arrest. Dragging me by the elbow, she rushes me down to the back of the store like I'm a naughty child who needs to be taken into the shadows for a good smack.

'I think I might be pregnant,' she hisses, her face white with fear.

'What? You're kidding? What is this city coming to? Don't *any* of the condoms work anymore?'

She bursts into a flood of tears. I am terrible in a crisis, which is odd given the way I lurch from one to another. You'd think I'd have picked up a few crisis management skills along the way.

I try to remember what people said to me when I had my pregnancy scare. As I recall, they were pretty darn thrilled for me, actually. Although, then again, I was never asked to sign a pre-nup declaring that I wouldn't drop an egg for five years.

I hold her against my woollen sweater as I've seen heroes do on romantic comedies, but I practically suffocate her and she has to fight her head out for breath.

'Don't you ever wash that thing?' she splutters, pulling bits of fluff out of her face.

'I don't have to answer that,' I tell her and she starts to smile, despite everything. I seize my advantage and begin an interrogation to get to the facts. 'Look Rebecca, are you sure about this? For a start, have you even done a proper test or anything? You don't want to be like me, the girl who cried foetus and ended up with egg on her face!'

Even as this stuff tumbles out of my mouth, I have a feeling that were Topsy here, she would have handled the whole situation with a lot more aplomb. She would have eased Rebecca into a bar and extracted the necessary information from her over a few daiquiris.

'What about the pre-nup thing? I thought you weren't allowed to fall pregnant in the first five years of marriage? Does Rob know?' I fumble. 'It is Vagina Man's, isn't it?'

Rebecca kicks me in the shins. 'I didn't fall, I was pushed, and of course it's his.'

'Ouch!' I squeal, rubbing my injured leg.

'Sorry about that, but what do you take me for?'

'Um, maybe we shouldn't go to that place, Okay?

The main thing is that you make certain that you really are pregnant before going into panic gear. Stress can put your cycle out.'

PS: Was I mature and together or what?

'I am stressed about the wedding but I've never missed my period before and I feel sick as a dog, Anna. I've been surfing the toilet all morning.'

'Well, oysters can do that,' I remind her.

'I don't eat seafood.'

'Right, well then, um . . .' I stammer, playing for time, but she can hear the resignation in my voice.

'I'm pregnant aren't I? I can feel it.'

'When were you due?' I ask, using a practical no-nonsense voice I've never heard myself use before. It is a voice my father used to use on my mother whenever she'd found out about one of his affairs. A voice that at once suggested he was a steady-as-you-blow kind of guy and Topsy was a hysterical ninny who needed gagging.

PS: He was half right.

'About two weeks ago,' she sniffles, dabbing at her eyes with one of the tissues. 'I had it marked down for that day when we met at that place with the eggplant bagels.'

I can't let a remark like this drop. 'Hang on, you mark your periods down? Where?'

'In my diary.'

'You mark your periods in a diary? You mean, along with what, lunch at Barneys, drinks at Bowery Bar, blood in knickers?' I stare at her as if she's just eaten a goldfish. 'Can't you see how weird you are?'

She looks as surprised as me. 'Don't you?'

'I don't even write my appointments down, Rebecca. Writing your periods down? You are seriously troubling, you do know that don't you? There are self-help books out there for girls like you.'

'Hang on, if you don't keep a record of your cycle, how do you know what mood you're going to be in?' she asks, equally as shocked as I am

I put my finger on my chin as if considering the question. 'Gee, let me think.' I slap her playfully on the arm. 'In case you've never noticed, I don't have moods, Rebecca. This is me, a PMS victim lurching like an emotional drunkard from one end of my cycle to another.'

She looks like she's about to cry. I try and think what I can do. 'So, basically what you are saying is that you haven't done an actual test yet?'

She shakes her head. 'No test.'

'Right,' I say, feeling suddenly all Topsy-ish and in control. 'Let's march you off to a pharmacy and get some champagne. I mean a pregnancy test. I bet this is nothing more than a case of pre-nup nerves,' I lie, as I take her by the hand and lead the way.

CHAPTER TWENTY-FOUR

Every year someone does a cover of that Carole King song, 'You Make Me Feel Like A Natural Woman!' and I wonder if I am the only girl barfing every time I hear it. The only natural thing about me is the enduring hair on my big toe which won't come off even with persistent waxing. I don't see what is so great about nature anyway.

For me, a declaration of love would be, 'You Make Me Feel Like An Artificially Enhanced Girl With A Huge Credit Zone'. The lyrics would go on and on, about how Mr Right makes me feel like a bleach-bathed, hairless, eyebrow-plucked, breast-lifted, lipo-sucked, credit-enriched uberbabe. You are, after all, what you feel.

Extract from the 'New York Girl' column of Anna Denier

Anna

In a crowded restroom in Saks Fifth Ave., Rebecca and I have been watching a pink line stay pink for like half an hour.

PS: Much to the chagrin and scarcely concealed horror of the attendant.

I am trying to be the voice of restraint which is a new voice for me and it still sounds slightly discordant and squeaky. 'Maybe the test is wrong? Okay, so it looks like a pink line in *this* light, but I bet if we take it outside it will go blue, just like those concealers that look fine at the counter and glow iridescently in the outdoor light.'

PS: Just because truth is destiny, it doesn't stop you living a lie.

Rebecca jabs me in the ribs with her elbow. Pregnancy seems to be triggering a lot of violence in her.

'Ouch!' I exclaim, rubbing my arm. 'I think you might have broken something.'

'The test is definitely positive, Anna. You know it, I know it, and the attendant here knows it.'

The attendant, as if to press the point home, starts spraying a toxic green liquid around us.

I can't keep up this voice of restraint forever. Of course it is positive. These tests are always positive. That's why I didn't do one myself. Why would any sane woman shell out the cost of a Wonderbra on a result that isn't going to turn your life upside down? Girls buy these tests to herald life-changing events, not to tell them what they want to hear.

I've heard that some girls keep the little sticks as a memento, but I am pleased to report that Rebecca casts hers into the feminine napkin disposal unit. A look of relief passes around the restroom staff.

'So that,' she announces ominously, 'is that.'

'Wow,' I say. 'You are really pregnant. You are really going to have a baby. God, I can't imagine you as a mom.'

She smiles sarcastically. 'Thanks Anna.'

I clasp my hands over my mouth. 'Sorry. It's just, well . . . someone's living inside you now.'

'Yeah, I guess,' she agrees, looking down at her belly with all the enthusiasm of a Business Class passenger being told they will have to travel coach. 'You make me sound like something off the *X-Files* though.'

'Topsy used to call me The Alien when she was pregnant,' I reveal. 'She actually wanted to name me Alien – thank God Jack stopped her. It was the biggest favour he ever did me.'

'Is that your dad then, Jack?'

'Yeah, haven't I told you about Jack before?'

'Not a thing. I didn't even know you had an official father. I guess I presumed that Topsy would be too advanced for a relationship. What's he like?'

'As his name suggests, he's a bit of a lad. Drinking lager, having a laugh and getting laid are the three L's according to my dad.'

'So, very in touch with his feminine side then?'

'You got it,' I agree, offering her a cigarette.

The restroom attendant approaches us with folded arms. 'No smoking,' she says in a voice that could freeze the Sahara. I only did it to wind her up anyway, but Rebecca puts five dollars in her tray as a pacifier.

'You shouldn't reward bad behaviour,' I scold, but Rebecca rolls her eyes.

'Look Anna, I don't know how Rob's going to take this. How will I tell him?' She's looking at me like goldfish in tanks look at you when they're hungry. A look that is both pleading and uncomprehending.

'You could hire one of those singing telegram people to—'

She frowns at me as if she's considering throwing me down the sanitary waste disposal unit after the stick.

'—or not,' I agree. So we start doing what women everywhere do when they're trying to think how they can face the rest of their lives. We start applying lipstick. Only I was checking out her reflection, and she was looking at mine, and between us we were making a mess of our liplines.

'Don't forget that people change,' I tell her. 'Once it's actually a *fait-accompli*, he might feel differently.'

'Men never change,' she argues. 'My mom always said, men are like shopping – there's never any change.'

'Yeah, well, Topsy told me that the only thing a woman should want from a man is a vaginal orgasm,' I pointed out. 'Mothers aren't exactly the greatest sages in the world. Otherwise we'd be worshipping *their* slippers. Hey, but you're going to be one. You'll have to start thinking up pithy aphorisms that your daughter or son can quote in restrooms as an adult.'

She studies me. 'You need to dab. Your lipline's all over the place.'

I start dabbing at my clownish lipline with a tissue.

'Rob *so* doesn't want to have kids,' she repeats. 'Sometimes I think it's almost the major motivational force in his life. His passion for *not* having kids.'

'Sort of ironic really, when you think of it. Given that he's a gynaecologist, I mean.'

She looks at me like she's about to squirt perfume in my eye again. 'I'll have to have an abortion,' she decrees, much louder than she means to. Suddenly the restroom seems to empty very quickly indeed. Maybe they thought she was talking about that minute or something. Maybe they thought I was about to pull surgical equipment out of my new shiny Prada and perform the procedure there and then.

'Let's have lunch and think about it a bit later,' I suggest quietly, giving her a smile that Topsy used to give me when I was sick. A kind of 'keep your distance when you sneeze' look of concern.

But Rebecca suddenly looks very determined and announces that she wants to go and check out the babywear section, and I don't really think I should dissent. But I do.

'Yeah right, of course you do. If you're going to have an abortion you want to make sure the foetus has the right accessories before you off it,' I joke. But she doesn't laugh.

So we go down to the baby section and check out all the smocking on the baby frocks, the brightly coloured mobiles and the soft toys. It is a bit like being in my apartment, really.

Rebecca starts hugging the bears first, so in a sense I am just a follower, just joining in, but it does kind of feel good. Over the course of the next half hour we hug every little furry friend in the place. From Winnie the Pooh to The Grouch. I can guarantee that there isn't a soft toy left loveless.

The sales staff, having established that we are merely cuddlers and not spenders, form themselves into a disapproving pack by the checkout, but we ignore them. We aah and ooh our faces off, in an orgy of soft-toy-cuddling previously unseen on Fifth Avenue.

And it doesn't take a genius to see that there is no way this woman is going to have an abortion. She is as gooey as a hot marshmallow and eventually the adult in me gets a grip and leads her upstairs to the restaurant where we gorge on talk of stag nights and hen nights and rooms in between.

I tell Rebecca about my dream. The one where I am being held prisoner inside an apartment with a black and white television and a sink full of dirty dishes while an all-male party rages next door. I tell her how I suspect that the revellers watch me behind a two-way mirror that divides my dull single-girl apartment from the all-guy fun next door.

I'm well into my stride by the time I notice that Rebecca's not listening at all. Not even politely pretending to, actually. 'If I tell him before the wedding,' she interjects, 'he'll break off the engagement. But if I tell him *after* the wedding, I'll feel like I trapped him,' she debates.

'Well yes, there is that. You could always tell him at the stag-stroke-hen night when he's feeling all celebratory and tribal,' I offer, only half jokingly. 'Give him an excuse to hand out cigars, anyway.'

But Rebecca falls on the idea as if it were a sword and she a Roman soldier. 'Of course. That's such a good idea.'

'Is it?'

But she's lost to reason. 'I love you!' she squeals as she dives into my lap. 'I love you, Anna. You're the best friend I've ever had.'

'Which is really, really flattering, honestly, but actually I'm not sure it is such a good idea.' I try to shift her back to her own seat. 'I don't think they're really big on lap dancing in Saks, Bec.'

'I just think it's such a wonderful idea – to tell him on his stag night.'

'Um, I mean, he might take it as a bit of a shock. See, I'm not certain that he'll be really prepared for fatherhood with all those *gatoy* lady-boys running around.'

'No, I think you're right,' she says determinedly. 'I'll tell him on his stag night. He's always in a good mood when he's drunk.'

I'm feeling very, very uneasy now. I'm glad she's

happy, obviously, but I'm not all together convinced that you should tell guys that you are pregnant on their stag night.

'There is also the possibility that the shock will kill him,' I argue, as I call out to a waiter and order another champagne cocktail for myself.

I need to be very, very smashed for this.

CHAPTER TWENTY-FIVE

Dear Anna,
Firstly, let me apologise for neglecting to reply to your letters
in the last year. Secondly, I have some news which I hope will
please you. I should have told you before you left but I was
worried how you'd take it. Fact is, I married Carol Thorn,
the assistant editor on my paper. My biological clock must
have finally gone off, hey? They say that men don't have a
biological clock but I think I must have. Carol gave birth to
Jon last month and I couldn't be happier. You have a brother.
The son I always wanted. I have given up work to be here
for him, to enjoy the relationship that Topsy prohibited me
having with you. This time round I don't want to miss a
thing. I hope you are planning a trip back here in the near
future to meet your brother. He is so adorable and I so want
the two of you to bond.
Your loving father,
The Ultimate Evil Bastard.

Letter to Anna Denier from Jack (The Lad) Denier

Anna

The son I always wanted.

I read the letter several times before tearing it into a thousand pieces and throwing it into the fire. The toys and I huddle together and watch it burn with a mixture of desolation and betrayal. I ring Topsy and rant about the evil of men and demand to know why she didn't put his testicles in the blender when she had the chance.

I hear her filing her nails. 'Perhaps he's finally tapped into the nurturer within?' she offers.

'Well fuck that.'

'I'm just happy he's happy,' she smarms.

'No you're not. You're pissed off and bewildered like me,' I insist.

'Topsy wants happiness and personal fulfilment for men and women alike, Eggnog.'

'I'm so in awe of your humanity I'm gagging.' My bile rises as I listen to the file scraping against her nails and my nerves.

'Maybe you should send your little half-brother a gift, Eggnog.'

'You mean like a blender or something?'

'Let it go, Eggnog,' she advises in a wheedling tone.

'Like he let me go, you mean?' Even I am astonished at the emotions surging up inside me, but there *is* a definite surge. Like that big tidal wave LA's always waiting for. I am afraid I am going to be carried out in a rip tide and lost at sea, clinging to my life-raft of resentment and self pity.

The UEB has also enclosed a photograph of himself holding his *wunderkind*, but my brother must have been trying to escape Jack's evil clutches because his image is nothing but a blur in a nautical theme hat. Far from making out any resemblance, I can't even make out a human form.

PS: The anchor on the hat is v. clear, though.

My father is grinning from ear to ear, holding up this blur with a cap on to the camera like the proudest man in the world. It occurs to me that perhaps my brother is another one of those chimeras who appear real but actually when you try to photograph them turn out not to be? Perhaps my father has bred his fantasy child, another God-Boy?

'All in all,' I tell the toys after I've hung up, 'it has been a bitch of a week.'

Sienna has been acting very oddly since I last

saw her, too. I know she went on a date because I heard the chanting and bell ringing that always precedes sex. When I asked her about her mystery man, though, she was really, really evasive. And that is so un-Sienna.

I wish people wouldn't get secretive like that when they fall in love. I really like hearing about my girl-friends' dates. Where's the fun in having girlfriends with active sex lives, if not for the vicarious sex you can have?

In complete contrast to Sienna I am as sexless as a girl can get at the moment. I toss and turn every night, tormented, amongst other things, by the dumb advice I gave to Rebecca about not telling Rob that he was going to be a father until the night of their combined stag-hen-bash.

'Did I seriously suggest that?' I ask at three am one morning, when I've rung her in an attempt to escape the guilt that's consuming me.

'Yes,' she murmurs drowsily.

I can hear Vagina Man snoring happily beside her as she whispers into the receiver, 'You convinced me it was the ideal time and you were right. Can I go back to sleep now?'

'No. No way, not until I talk you out of this insanity.'

It is twenty minutes before I acquiesce, or rather

admit defeat, having failed in my mission to talk her into breaking it to Rob a tad earlier than his own stag night. Boy, was he going to hit the roof. Couldn't she see that?

I ask her to imagine for a moment how Vagina Man might feel, being told on the night of his last stand with the guys that his intended – the one he had agreed to marry despite her refusal to sign a pre-nup swearing off conception for five years – was *already* in the family way?

But she's nodded off.

Boy, do I feel responsible. I really like Rebecca and I really didn't like the idea that she is about to ruin her life – based on the advice of Anna Denier.

I confide the burden of my guilt to Mark when he phones to see if I've relented on my decision not to see him anymore. His laughter rings down the phone like a ten mil shot of Valium.

'Don't laugh,' I tell him, even though I am actually praying that he will never stop laughing, not ever. He has the coolest laugh in the world and I curl up in bed and smile all over my body. Even my hips are smiling, which is amazing given that they are the most reliably glum part of my anatomy.

'He is going to flip!' he states. 'Shit, he's going to do back flips.' Then he laughs some more at the very thought of it. Vagina Man is one of those guys who prides himself on a steadiness of temperament, a phlegmatic nature. The image of him back flipping is kind of jarring, even without the added plus that Rob's body is made for rolling. Not that he is fat, let's just say that he's on the cuddly-bear side rather than the athletic.

'Rob's pretty rabid on the issue of not having kids till later on. Not that he doesn't want kids, he does. Talks about what it would be like to have a son all the time. No, he definitely digs kids, but having the bomb dropped on his stag night? Man! She can't be serious?'

'Oh, she's serious,' I assure him. 'I can't talk her out of it. She's convinced that the combination of lady-boys, cigars and copious amounts of alcohol will put him in the mood.'

'It will put him in the mood, sure, but it won't be the mood to be told that he's a father-to-be.'

'That's what I told her!'

'I love it when we agree.'

I let his remark pass. 'What's worse is that she credits me with coming up with the hideous plan.'

Sitting there in my bed, curled up like a kitten, hugging The Count, I am getting turned on just by the sound of his breath coming down the phone line when he isn't speaking. A smile of utter contentment spreads across my face. It is just like old times. Only without the really important part. The spooning thing.

'Anna?'

'Yeah?'

'I thought you'd hung up. You went quiet.'

'I'm still here,' I whisper, afraid I'll disclose how desperate and horny I'm feeling.

'I need to see you Anna,' he whispers back.

I nod but I can't speak.

'Are you there still?'

'U-huh.'

'Anna, I hate this being apart thing,' he groans.

I hate it too. But I have principles to uphold, or something very close to principles anyway. 'Mark, please don't. You know I can't. We want different things.'

'So do the Arabs and the Israelis, the Catholics and the Protestants. They still meet to talk about it.'

'Only cause they get bombed if they don't.'

'Plus, there's something I've got to tell you. What are you doing tomorrow?'

'Mark, don't do this. We want different things.'

'I've got to tell you something,' he repeats. 'You might not be thrilled but you need to know so we can put all this behind us. Topsy agrees. She had a go at me for not telling you sooner.'

I feel suddenly annoyed. 'Gee, how sweet of Topsy!

I live for my mother to have a go at my lovers.' I hear the bitterness in my voice and hate myself for it.

'Are we?'

'Are we what?'

'Lovers. You just said that you live for your mother to have a go at your lovers. You didn't say *ex*-lovers, just lovers.'

'A slip of the tongue,' I explain, biting my lower lip. 'Ouch.'

'I'd love you to slip your tongue into my mouth right now.'

I close my eyes and imagine doing just that.

'Do you have any idea how much I'm missing you, Anna? Even Mom is at me to get back with you. Her and Topsy are thick as thieves these days. They're always on the phone together.'

'Fantastic,' I sneer, as sarcastically as I can, which isn't very sarcastically now that my lip has swollen up after the nip I gave it earlier. It came out sounding rather lispy and cute, actually.

'I love you,' he says.

I fight against the urge to say the same to him. The words I've never actually brought myself to say. Principles, I tell myself. Remember your principles, Anna Denier. 'You mean you love my reproductive capabilities,' I correct, back on track.

'Crap. I'd love you with or without a uterus. I don't

care. I just want us to be together. This is madness. Don't cut me off like this, Anna. We can talk about the kid issue later on down the track.'

'No, we can't. That's just it. We can't talk about it later on down the track. You still don't get it. There *is* no later on down the track for me.' I hammer in the last of my points with a rivet gun of a tone. 'I don't want kids up the track, down the track, or on the track.

'•I never want to be impregnated.

'•I never want to struggle on the subway with a baby buggy.

'•I never want to do school runs.

'•I never want to get woken up at night to change a diaper. Actually, I never want to change a diaper, even in the daylight hours.

'•I never want stretch marks, saggy tits or hand prints on my clothes.'

I can think of a thousand other things I don't want but I also don't want to sound too ridiculous.

'But what about me? Maybe I can be like Arnold Schwarzenegger in *Junior*,' he jokes. 'They're saying that it is physically possible for men to have children now. We have the technology,' he teases.

'Don't be flip.'

'Well shit, Anna, you paint a pretty bleak picture of motherhood,' he says.

'Well it's a pretty bleak business,' I tell him, sounding ridiculously stiff.

'It wouldn't have to be like that,' he reasons. 'I'm sure Topsy didn't go through all that.'

'Bingo! You're damn right she didn't and that's why I'm like I am. I missed out on all that misery other kids got to inflict on their mothers. It's warped me.'

'I like you warped,' he says in his sexiest drawl.

'Look Mark, face it, you want kids and I don't. It's what's known as an irreconcilable difference. Now you're trying to whitewash your needs. But one day you might decide that you want kids, desperately. More than you want me even and I just don't want to go to that place.'

The line goes quiet for a full minute. I can hear his breathing and I feel like I could listen to it all night long.

'Truth is destiny,' I mutter, needing to fill the silence, wanting to throw something into the void between us. Instead, I start talking about Jack. 'My father had another baby. His name's Jon and he's given up work to care for him full time because he doesn't want to miss a thing.' There, I've said it.

'I thought his testicles had been liquidised.'

'Topsy never got round to it, actually. She was probably afraid of breaking a nail. He wants to have the relationship with Jon that he didn't have with me, can you believe it? The Blur, that's what I call him, is going to get the relationship with Jack that should have been mine!' I want Mark to reach down the phone line and hold me against his chest.

'You're upset. I'm coming over,' he threatens.

'No, don't do that,' I insist, frightened by how much I want him to do exactly that. 'I need some space.'

'There's plenty of space here.'

But it's not space that I want, it's him. And that will never work. It is pointless to drag this whole breaking up thing out. 'I'll call you soon,' I promise in the voice of a casting director who has no intention of doing any such thing.

'How soon?' he presses.

'What, you want a time?'

'That's right. You don't want me to languish by the phone do you?'

I laugh, relenting slightly. 'I'll see you at Rebecca and Rob's Goodbye to Single Life Forever night. And don't forget, you can't say anything to Rob about Rebecca being pregnant, okay? You have to promise me.'

'Only if you promise to see me before then.'

'Hey, that's blackmail.'

'Well, I'll try to keep it a secret anyway, of course. Just that seeing you might put it way back in the darkest chambers of my mind, that's all.' I can tell that he's smiling on the other end of the line, teasing me in the nicest possible way.

But I stay firm, true to my principles. 'I'm really busy. I've got deadlines.'

'Just coffee?' he pleads.

We set a date for three days' time.

Knowing I'm going to see Mark soon doesn't help me to sleep, though. I'm worrying about Rebecca taking my dumb advice as gospel. Given that my upbringing was free of religious tuition of any description, I don't know how I got this overdeveloped guilt gland. Maybe it is a recessive gene? I think Topsy's parents were Episcopalians.

Whatever the antecedents, my guilt manifests into this huge, unwieldy force. Almost a physical form, a shadowy presence roaming the apartment. Sienna says that she can see it and offers to do an exorcism. 'It's putting its feet up like it's here for a long, long visit, Anna,' she warns.

I feel intimidated by my guilt, afraid that my advice will cause terrible harm to innocent people – Rebecca mostly. I have vision of my guilt breaking out into the West Village with a spray can, to graffiti my sins everywhere.

Topsy Denier's daughter advises ex-boyfriend's ex-girlfriend to conceal pregnancy from Vagina Man!'

CHAPTER TWENTY-SIX

I approach the future like I approach my wardrobe — that is, I try not to. I should get some direction. Get one of those capsule wardrobe thingamees together, with matching colours, blah, blah, blah.

But I never do.

As long as that size six aqua and orange micro mini from Jean Paul Gaultier still fits, I don't have to worry about tomorrow. I am still asking the questions that my married friends answered years ago. Like, what do I want to be when I grow up? Um . . . a size six with pert breasts and perfect skin. Where do I sign up?

The only thing I know for sure is that I don't want to give up on the size six within me; she's still inside me, I'm sure of it, and if she does decide to come out, I'll be here with that micro mini to welcome her.

Extract from the 'New York Girl' column of Anna Denier

Anna

Like some kind of harbinger of doom, my mother bangs on the door the next morning at the ungodly hour of ten am. Totally unannounced and bloody demanding as usual. 'I'm taking you out to breakfast,' she announces imperiously.

'Are you mad?' I ask in my croaky, just-got-woken-up voice and my putrid, haven't-cleaned-my-teeth breath. I'm already wearing sunglasses as I stick a cigarette on my lower lip and consider lighting it just to annoy her.

'Didn't we set it up?' She pouts when I don't fly into a lather of enthusiasm. I shake my head and grunt. She flutters her remarkably long eyelashes, pretending to be truly surprised. 'Oh Topsy can be such a scatter brain,' she concedes, with a trademark stroke of her immaculate hair.

I make this really peeved sighing sound that I'd picked up from the checkout operators in London. Then I look her up and down – tight black jersey dress, patent-black Chanel mules, teamed with matching handbag and pearl accessories. The stand-ard stuff.

'Love, love, love the hair, Eggnog. What have you done to it?'

Before I can answer she's thrust a bottle of Bollinger into my hands explaining that we have something spectacular to celebrate and that I have to get dressed, get upbeat and get out of the flat.

'Aubergine is it?'

'What?'

'The colour.'

I am bewildered. My mother likes my hair? What is this?

'It looks lovely, really brings out the violet in your eyes. Very sexy. Where?'

'What?'

'Who created the look darling?'

'Robert Kree on Bleecker.'

'What fun. Now throw on some clothes, we're off to celebrate.' I blink like a rabbit caught in the headlights of a Juggernaut until she claps her hands in front of my face, 'Chop, chop!'

'Is this something to do with that baby? Because I am resolutely committed to not celebrating his Blur.'

'Blur?'

'The Blur, it's my name for my step-brother.'

'I wouldn't waste Bolly on Jack or his son. Anyway, Jack's more a beer man.'

'I am irritated by the hour, her demand that I 'chop, chop' and, well, the sheer Topsyness of it all, but my curiosity is piqued. 'So what are we celebrating then?'

'*You*, Eggnog. We are facing the fact that you are in love with Mark, the man of your dreams, and the fact that you are phoning him now to tell him you have come to your senses.' She gives me a peck on the nose, and I can just imagine the Rudolf mark she's left behind.

'Are you on a high dose of that date rape drug, what is it? Rohypnol?' I call out to her back as she picks her way gingerly through the detritus of my apartment and opens the tiny balcony door. 'Because there are calls to have that banned, you know.'

She looks around dubiously. 'It's so musty in here. How often does your cleaner come?'

I stick the champagne in the refrigerator and get a whiff of something that went off a very long time ago. 'I don't have a cleaner,' I yell out to her as I bash my head repeatedly on the freezer handle in the hope that I'll knock myself out and be whizzed off to the comparatively serene realm of the Emergency Room.

She is passing the telephone to me as I walk

back into the room rubbing the lump. 'Come on now, give him a ring. You know you want to,' she cajoles.

Standing before her, my eggplant coloured hair sticking out on one side like the flag of a recently formed terrorist group, and wearing my Trailer-Trash night-dress, I know I am no match for her. But just the same, a girl's got to do etcetera. I place my hands on my hips defiantly and spell the word. 'N-O!'

'Just for Topsy, Eggnog?' She wobbles her lower lip.

'Stop interfering.'

Her lower lip curls down even lower. 'Don't du want to make widdle Topsy happy, Eggnog?'

Oh dear. We're in the baby-voice zone. This is going to be worse than I thought. 'No,' I repeat, firmly.

She wrinkles her tiny nose-job prettily and gestures to the hell hole of my apartment. 'Topsy weally, weally, cares for her widdle Eggnog.'

It is useless. When Topsy is determined – well, I think you can imagine. And granted, she probably does have more enchanting places to visit than my apartment. Even I can think of a thousand more enchanting places I'd rather be. The dentist even. At least she keeps her room clean. Face it, my life is trash. Since leaving Mark I haven't had the will to clean. The will for anything much, really.

The desk area looks particularly incriminating now that I notice it. Actually, you can't see the computer or the desk as they are hidden under the pile up of John's Pizzeria pizza boxes, HSF Chinese take-out containers and screwed up bits of paper. I really hope they never want to do one of those 'At Home With Anna Denier' pieces on me.

I hold my ground out of habit. 'News Flash Topsy – Mark is in love with my womb, not me. Endorse that!' I dare her.

She rolls her eyes like a screen actress of the silent era. 'He adores you, Eggnog.' She comes over and takes my face in her hands. 'Apartment like a tip, dress-sense of a refugee, organisation skills of a hamster – the man worships you. He's successful, good looking and wised up to his own feelings. Get a problem, girlfriend.'

'I don't need to get a problem,' I remind her, pulling away. 'I have you.'

A few minutes later and she is in absolute control, passing me items of clothing to put on as we continue to thrash out the Mark-versus-principle issue.

Out of habit, I am taking the proffered apparel and pulling it over my head without argument. Before I realise what I've done I am looking incredible, wearing the outfit she bought me a few weeks back on our shopping expedition to Barneys. The day she set me up with Mark.

'Fine state of affairs isn't it, that Topsy – *I'll Have Mine On The Rocks!* – Denier, is persuading her own daughter to sacrifice herself on the altar of a man's need to reproduce his DNA?' I parry.

'Good headline,' she concedes, tipping her head to one side thoughtfully. 'I'd use it myself – if it were true. You need to sit down and let him say what he needs to say, Eggnog. As usual, you're firing off, all cannons blazing without a discernible target in sight.'

'What is your problem?' I ask.

'Where do I start?' she inquires sarcastically.

'Very funny – *not.*'

'Why are you so down on your poor little brother Jon?'

I know I'm being sidelined but I turn around, holding up my hair so Topsy can do up my zipper. 'Anyway, it's all your fault the way I'm so screwed up about men. You wouldn't let Jack have a proper relationship with me.'

'Oh save it.'

'Nothing was ever good enough for Topsy queen of everything. He couldn't fold a diaper, rock me in my cradle or even burp me to your satisfaction. Face it, you hounded him out of his natural yearning for a relationship with me. And now he's going to have that relationship with The Blur. A kid with the most stupid taste in caps I've ever seen.'

'He's only a few weeks old, darling.'

'Still.'

During my speech, Topsy has passed me a wet face-cloth, and as I wipe it across my face I feel the sting of tears banking up at the backs of my eyes.

'Don't forget that it was *me* who urged you to go and stay with Jack in London, Eggnog. You were the one who didn't want to go.'

'Only because I knew you wanted to get rid of me,' I remind her.

'Eggnog. How can you say that?'

'Um, gee, let me think,' I say in mock ignorance, putting my finger on my chin as if considering my answer. 'Because it's true, possibly?'

She chooses to ignore my sarcasm. 'Where is your brush?'

'On the desk.'

She wanders over and tackles Pizza Box Mountain. 'Granted, I wasn't a natural born mother, but since the moment you entered my life you have been my only true love. And besides, as if I would care how anyone tied a diaper.'

'You don't *tie* a diaper, Topsy. You pin them, or

use those sticky things on the side,' I inform her, as if I know masses about such things.

She is rummaging about my desk so I can't see her face but she sounds kind of hurt. I don't think I've ever seen my mother upset. 'Anyway, neither of us ever *had* to change a diaper. We had a nanny darling, a haughty little thing from England who thought Topsy Denier was an unfit mother. Well, maybe I was. But as for burping you? It never occurred to Jack to burp anyone other than himself.' She giggles girlishly at her little joke.

There is a tear running down my left cheek, carrying the cargo of last night's mascara with it. What is it with MAC mascara that nothing found in the medicine cabinet will shift it? But weep, and every dollop you've applied in the last five years is flushed out.

'Well he's burping Jon now and apparently finding it very rewarding,' I sniffle.

'Well rah-rah for him. So he's finally discovered the joy of parenthood. Big deal. That doesn't reflect on you, Eggnog. It comes to some people late in life and to some people not at all. That was the problem with our generation, we made our choices before we knew all our options.' She unearths the brush and brandishes it like an Academy Award. For a second she gives the impression that she's about to start thanking all the little people.

That, or give me a spanking.

'I still needed a father,' I snap, as a surge of anger reigns in my tears. 'He would have loved me more if it wasn't for you. How do you think it felt, hearing you talk about how his testicles should be liquidised over breakfast every morning?'

Topsy turns me around and starts brushing my hair. It feels divine, just like it did when I was small. And despite the banked up resentment I feel towards her, my anger drains away with each successive stroke. No one could brush my hair like her.

Gently, she takes hold of the roots and teases the knots, carefully and virtually painlessly, from the ends. Nanny had always tugged the knots and made me cry. 'Shush child,' she would hiss, ripping out my roots. 'Don't fuss.' I always loved it when Topsy brushed my hair.

'It wasn't anything to do with me or you, Eggnog. Your father was a born herd impregnator.'

I roll my eyes.

'I'm pleased for him that he's finally allowing himself to enjoy a mature relationship. When I was with him his idea of monogamy was screwing one woman at a time.'

'Oh right, and like you didn't know that before you married him?'

She ignores my remark as well she should. I'm

being a complete bitch. She just makes Jack's neglect of me sound so reasonable.

'My patience for him ran out the day I walked in to find him screwing that wretched nanny virtually in front of you, Eggnog. I may be a liberal, but I sure as hell wasn't going to allow him to get away with that one. I threw her out on the spot. I only let him hang around a few more years because you adored him so much. That was why I gave up my acting career and started writing books. I could write from home and work my schedule around you.'

I swallow hard. 'I never knew that about you. You wanted to be an actor?' She has passed me the eyeliner and a compact mirror while making this revelation and in shock I have drawn a long black line running from one end of my face to the other. I look like the bride of Frankenstein.

'I'm sure it was all for the best,' she answers crisply. 'I love my life!'

'How old was I?' I ask, my voice childlike and strangled, the product of vocal chords frozen with hurt.

'Five.'

I swallow. Nauseous. The image of myself watching my father screw Nanny Carter. Erk. And I can't remember it at all – I must need loads and loads of therapy. 'Did I know what they were doing?'

Topsy keeps on brushing, sweeping the hair from the nape of my neck in a gesture so tender it makes me feel ashamed of my harshness towards her. 'You didn't look that interested in the two of them. You were busy in the annexe off the living room while they were at it. Playing with your Lego. Building a house for Action Man,' she assures me, kissing me lightly on the head. 'I don't think you were aware of what they were up to.'

'Action Man saw Jack doing ... with ... Nanny Carter? I had no idea.' Topsy wipes the offending black mark from my face with the cloth. 'That must have been why I got rid of Action Man. I wondered what happened to him. It was probably a mercy killing. I probably thought he'd never recover from what he saw.'

'Not quite. Action Man was on a shelf while you were building the den for him. I grabbed him without thinking and hit her with it.'

'Oh God, did I see?'

'You cheered. You were so proud of Action Man that day. You never liked Nanny Carter. So I gave Jack a whack on the back of the head as well for good measure. Unfortunately, Action Man died in the pursuit of duty. His head snapped off.'

'Pity it wasn't Nanny Carter's,' I say as I look into

the famous blue pond eyes of the world's most famous feminist theorist ever and see in them, for the first time, not the diva of talk shows who demanded and had it all, but the woman who had come to her role as mother unnaturally. And done the best she could with the limited material available.

Topsy was in her mid-twenties when she gave birth to me, the same age as I am now. I suddenly think of Leda and Charles as I imagine my mother, fired with her beliefs and ideals, standing on podiums, going on chat-shows, and lobbying politicians with me in a papoose. And I compare the image with me. My pathetic ideals are far less noble, revolving as they do around the never-ending search for something to give me a cleavage, the pursuit of cellulite-free thighs, the quest for the latest Gucci shoe and, most important of all, the drive to banish my body of hair. I feel really insignificant and really, really selfish.

'Did you plan me?' I ask.

'Darling, I'm no better at planning than you. And besides, don't you think all the best things happen when you're least prepared? How could I ever have planned for something as monumentally life changing as you, Eggnog?'

I want to throw myself into her arms but I force myself to ask the *un*-askable, gagging the part of me that doesn't want to know. 'If you weren't ready, why didn't you have an abortion? I mean, you don't have to answer, but surely you thought about it?'

A smile plays about her mouth. 'Everyone asked that at the time. But firstly, your father would have taken me to court if I had. Despite his flaws, he did want you, Eggnog. *Does* want you. And you know, it never occurred to me as a real option. I loved Jack, and in his own way he loved me, and you were the perfect expression of that love.'

'You loved him?' I'd never heard her say those words about my father.

'To distraction,' she promises. 'To the exclusion of reason. And you have to understand, Eggnog, your father really was thrilled that I was carrying you.' She laughs and turns back to face me. 'That house in San Francisco smelt of cigars for years.'

I imagine her then as she must have felt, pregnant in her twenties, stumbling into the unexpected responsibility of caring for another little person. Okay, so she hasn't been a mother in the Marion-of-*Happy-Days* kind of way. She hasn't been an earth mother who lived to bake wholemeal bread. She is a different sort of mother.

She is the sort of mother who taught me to question the status quo, to confront what I don't believe and to challenge what I think is wrong. Even when it is her. And she taught me that it is alright to feel bewildered by things that no one else seems to have a problem with. It is alright to be myself. And I realise then, in that moment, that despite the hype, despite the madness, Topsy has always been there for me, in her own glamorous, champagne swilling, life's-one-long-publicity-party way.

I'd never realised that, partly because she had never martyred herself like the mothers of my friends. When it mattered, though, Topsy was always there. Maybe not holding the bucket, but reading a story, telling me about her day, or most memorably lugging in those large terra-cotta pots from the garden.

'These are geraniums, Eggnog,' I can still hear her explaining, struggling to drag the massive pots into my sick room when I had mumps. 'Geraniums are a girl's best friend, Eggnog. They'll hang in there for you even when you're too depressed to water them, too busy to remember how much their beauty means to you.'

As a whole flood of memories comes washing up on the shore line of my consciousness, I fall into her arms and sob for all the wasted years I've spent resenting her and blaming her. And even though I know she must be thinking that my makeup is going to leave pink marks on her black frock, she holds me against her tiny bosom and strokes my errant head of hair.

'Can we open the champagne now?' she pleads.

CHAPTER TWENTY-SEVEN

Parents are embarrassing. They belong to an era you've left behind. The era of childhood behaviour and needs. Notwithstanding all the love and care they gave you as a child, you still want them to walk on the other side of the street when you grow up.

You ask yourself – did they always talk this loud? Did they always dress like this? Did they always go on about stuff this way. But the worst part about parents when you grow up is that you realise they are human. You realise that they made dumb decisions, that they hurt themselves as much as they hurt you, and slowly you grow to see that they are neither the idols nor the demons you set them up as.

Which is all the more reason to make them walk on the other side of the street.

Extract from the 'New York Girl' column of Anna Denier

Anna

Topsy and I are still in a state of acute bonding when Charles arrives with his baby slung around his front like a really noisy prosthetic belly. Leda is howling. Topsy and I aren't much better, it has to be said.

He seems in a bit of a panic when he speaks. 'Have you seen Sienna?' he asks. 'She's not downstairs. I . . . um . . . thought she might be here?'

Confused as to why he'd want to see Sienna, I shake my head vaguely.

'Do you mind if I wait here?' he asks.

When I tell him that it's fine, he sits down and looks nervous, guilty even. I am wearing my saggy T-shirt with the words Trailer Park Trash emblazoned across the front. What I once thought a highly ironic statement in night-wear now seems, well . . . kind of appropriate.

I'd changed back into the T-shirt around the time Topsy decided that I should be put back to bed, wrapped up in my quilt and 'mothered'. It was too beautiful a suggestion to disobey.

I allowed her to tuck me in and settled down to reading the instructions to a new cellulite disappearing cream I'd bought the other day, while Topsy went off to prepare me some Earl Grey tea. The fact that my kitchen had seen far more Grey in its time than Earl, didn't occur to me at first. The whole idea just seemed too splendid to spoil with reality.

However, the splendid plan had gone all pear-shaped when Topsy opened the shutters that shielded the rest of my apartment from my kitchenette and discovered, not the implements for tea-making, but a kind of cockroach nursing home.

She came back to drag me off to breakfast but I was pretty stuck on the idea of my T-shirt, and so she decided that we may as well drink the Bolly after all and cheer ourselves up a bit.

Topsy takes over the situation like the mistress that she is. 'Would you like a glass of champagne, Charles?' she asks after I introduce them.

'No thanks, not while I'm feeding.' He points to his screaming bundle.

Topsy and I look at one another and decide we probably shouldn't ask, but after two mugs of champagne, what the hell. We aren't really possessed of much self-control.

I plough in first. 'If you don't mind me asking, Charles . . . um, how are *you* feeding the baby. What

I mean is, you're not taking mammary-inducing hormones are you?' I fall apart and scream with the hilarity of it all, forcing Topsy to step in.

'What Anna means is that we can see how you can give little Leda a bottle, but how can a mug of champagne affect her feeding? Given that the milk isn't being dispensed by your body.'

Charles shakes his head as if we are fools. 'I need all my faculties, don't I?' he points out, as if we are like totally drunk and brain dead. Which perhaps we are.

'Would you like me to hold Leda? Topsy offers.

'No, it's okay, she starts squealing if I take her out.'

Topsy and I do that silent mother-daughter thing, where we look at one another and concur again. 'Well, if you don't mind me pushing the point Charles, your daughter is squealing her head off now!'

'This?' he asks, indicating his daughter's howling. 'This is nothing. You should hear her at night. She bawls the apartment building down.'

'Give her to me,' Topsy insists.

Charles looks at her for a minute, seeming to debate whether to run, but then, like any partially sane man would faced with the diva of having-it-all-and-then-some, hands his daughter over into the perfectly manicured hands of my mother.

'There, there little one. You didn't like being stuck in the nasty man's pouch did wu?' she coos, looking down into Leda's face.

Miraculously, Leda coos back. Well, maybe she doesn't make an the actual cooing noise, but she goes quiet. 'Take her little fist,' Topsy orders Charles, who is utterly mesmerised by her powers to silence his daughter. He does as she instructs and holds his daughter's tiny fist.

'There, now stick it in her mouth.'

I watch, struck by the ceremony as he guides the fist into the tiny bow-shaped mouth. Like a suction cap, Leda sucks on it for all she's worth.

'You can do that when she's in the pouch. They like the sucking, see, it soothes them. And if you can get them to take their own fist it's so much better than a pacifier – they always get lost. You can even dip her hand in champagne if you like.'

'Or not,' I argue, sensibly throwing Topsy an off-camera stern look.

'So your wife isn't breast-feeding her then?' I ask, curious as to why Charles is delivering wood with his daughter in a pouch.

'Life-partner,' he corrects pointedly. 'Well, she was expressing it at first, but it all got too much. She's a spray-can artist, see, and she can't take Leda to the studio with her. Not with all those chemicals. Besides, she's not as into caring for Leda as I am.' He looks agitated. 'Do you think Sienna will be long?'

My curiosity is aroused now. 'Why do you want to see Sienna, she doesn't have a fireplace does she?'

He stares at the floor. 'No, see that's the thing. We were . . . are . . . sort of going out on a date.'

'Date?'

'On a date.'

'Together?'

He nods.

'But you're married, you've got a wife,' I remind him, thinking of Jack dating other women with me in a pouch.

'Life-partner,' he corrects.

'Well, same thing. Worse really. Life is forever, a wife is just for the term of the marriage.'

'We're not getting on,' he says, looking down at Leda.

'You've just had a baby together. Things are bound to be a bit out of gear.'

Topsy looks at me. I realise I sound like a counsellor and try to shut up. Suddenly I'm more confused than ever about this guy, who would take his wife to hospital on the subway and yet seems to all intents and purposes to be grafted to his daughter. And now he is fooling around with Sienna, one of my best friends. I suddenly remember the bells I'd heard ringing in her apartment. 'How long has this been going on?'

His answer is to blush.

For once I am too stunned to say something stupid. Topsy cajoles him into half a mug of champagne after all, and passes me Leda, now fast asleep, sucking on her little fist. She is awesome. I wonder briefly if I am the sort of girl who could give up stuff for a baby. I'd tried to give up coffee once but didn't make it through the day. And cigarettes, well, I am more likely to make it up Everest. I try to imagine Mark giving up work to care for his son or daughter.

'Guess what?' Topsy squeals suddenly, clapping her hands together.

'Careful, you'll wake the baby,' I shush.

'Your lovely Topsy has the perfect answer to your dilemma with Mark,' she promises. 'It just came to me,' she says, pausing to sip champagne. 'Why don't you put your eggs on ice?'

Notwithstanding our Topsy-daughter bonding session, I'm cynical by nature of her motivation to get me to do anything. Even though it is an idea I had once toyed with myself I'm not going to let her think I am prepared to take her suggestion seriously.

'You mean so that you can ride the publicity gravy train?'

She lets out a shocked squawk. 'I'll never tell a

soul. Not even Mark, if you want. I just think you should think about it that's all.'

I pretend to consider the question carefully. 'I don't think that's the solution, anyway. I *have* thought of putting some eggs aside, but just because I do, that doesn't necessarily mean I'll ever want to activate them. It would just be getting his hopes up.'

'Ever's a long time,' Charles interjects.

'Well it was clearly too long as far as your commitment to your life-partner was concerned,' I point out sarcastically.

'He's right,' Topsy persists.

Charles and Topsy look knowingly at one another as if they've found a common cause. Charles takes this as his cue. 'Yeah, look at me, I never wanted kids. It was always Klarissa that was banging on about having a kid. It was her that stopped using her cap.'

'Oh please, and you couldn't work out how to put on a condom,' I snarl. I'm very annoyed with him actually, both for ganging up on me with Topsy and for dating Sienna. I don't want to see her hurt.

'No, well . . . I don't know. I withdrew.'

I can't resist the sarcasm. 'Oh well, that clearly worked, didn't it?'

'Maybe it was fate,' he says, taking his daughter back from me. 'I didn't want kids but I haven't got *kids*. I've got Leda and she's the best thing that's ever happened to me.' He strikes a pose reminiscent of those Communist leaders they made all those naff statues of. Proud and ridiculous in one – his child clutched to his chest, his face twisted with determination.

Then Sienna walks in. Charles jumps up and the look that passes between the two of them says it all.

Sienna looks at me guiltily. 'So you know then?' she says.

'I guess truth is destiny,' I state glibly.

CHAPTER TWENTY-EIGHT

Dear Jon,

Welcome to the Denier line. I am your big sister. I didn't actually have time to prepare for my new role, I didn't even get to audition actually, landing the part through nepotism rather than talent. I hope I'll do. I'm a bit worried, actually, that I'm not mature enough for someone else to look up to, see. Our father sent me a photograph of you, but it makes you look like a blur in a cap, so I've asked for another. I hope that you are really good looking and kind and smart etc. because girls always prefer those qualities in a guy. I'm going to try and get to London soon so I can meet you, but in the meantime I am sending you a new cap. Let's face it, the other one was a bit wussy. First big sister tip by the way: matters of a sartorial nature are best not left to Dad.

In the meantime, I'll try and grow up a bit.

Lots of love,

Anna

Letter from Anna Denier to her brother Jon (The Blur) Denier

Anna

Rebecca and I are having a set lunch in a restaurant on Columbus and I'm telling her about Topsy's suggestion that I freeze my eggs when she hits the roof.

'What?' she cries, as if I've proposed deep frying them in batter.

'That way I'm not closing myself off to possibilities in the future,' I explain calmly.

Rebecca shakes her head emphatically. 'It sounds like a publicity stunt to me.' And then she sneers uncharacteristically.

'No, Topsy said she wouldn't tell a soul,' I insist, knowing how naive I must sound.

Rebecca's fork stalls in mid-air. 'And you believe her?' She shakes her head disdainfully.

I was hoping she'd be delighted, given all my angst over my relationship with Mark. I thought she'd see it as a potential happily-forever-after scenario for everyone.

'I think it's a very bad idea,' she states firmly, as

if that should be the end of the discussion, and goes back to eating.

But I long for consensus on this. 'Actually, I think it's a really, really good idea.'

'Humph.'

I ignore her tone, putting it down to hormones. 'It's not as if the idea hadn't occurred to me anyway.'

'Look Anna, this doesn't seem very thought out to me. Have you even spoken to Mark about this?'

'Of course not. Why would I speak to Mark? We're not even together anymore, not officially.'

'Presumably it'll cost money?'

'See, the most seductive part of it is, Topsy's offering to pay for it.'

She holds her fork up as if it is some kind of satellite dish that is helping her brain to work. 'I think Mark has a right to know,' she insists.

'Well I don't, and they're my eggs we're talking about. I don't know why you are being so negative about this, anyway. Pregnancy has made you very cynical,' I scold teasingly.

'You asked my opinion and I *don't* think it's a good idea,' she says. 'In fact I think it's a very *bad* idea. The worst.' She is looking at me in a very serious grown-up kind of way, as if she's about to reveal something shocking. 'Look Anna, have you considered that you're diving into this because your mother's pushing you?'

'You really think Topsy has any sway over me?'

'Why don't you at least see what Mark's got to say?'

'Why would I want to see what he's got to say?' I snap. 'It's *my* body.'

'But isn't this the reason you guys fell out? Because you don't want kids and you think he does?'

She's got me there. 'That's true,' I concede, taking a sip of my wine, 'but I don't want to talk to him until I've decided. I don't want to get his hopes up. Nothing's definite.'

She nods thoughtfully and goes back to eating for a bit then suddenly it occurs to her. 'Won't it hurt? I mean, removing eggs from your ovaries, it doesn't sound like my idea of fun.'

I burst into a round of canned laughter. 'Hurt? Are you for real?' I jeer. 'Rebecca, you're having a baby in eight months' time, unless Vagina Man decides to kill you first for misuse of his sperm that is.'

'That's different.'

'Face it. Childbirth is way more painful than anything. Do you know that experiments prove that if a guy had to go through labour, he would die!' I can see she is rattled by this so I press home my advantage. 'Although I don't know how they measured that statistic unless they killed some poor guy in a lab experiment or something,' I hazard, stuffing a piece of bread in my mouth.

'I haven't thought about the pain,' she admits.

I can see she's worried but it's best that she faces facts now. At least that way she won't do something crazy like opt for a natural birth or a Lamaze method, or something kooky and masochistic like that.

'Well you should,' I advise her. 'I hear labour makes having your legs waxed look like a massage. And all I'm talking about is the careful removal of a few teeny weenie eggs, which is like nothing compared to the pushing out of a seven-pound dumpling.'

'I'm going to tell him,' she announces out of the blue, dropping her fork with a clatter. Everyone else in the place turns around as, zombie-like, she repeats her threat, only louder this time. 'I'm going to call him now and tell him.'

The thought of Mark finding out about my plan to freeze my eggs from Rebecca shocks the pants off me. 'No way! If anyone's going to tell him, it's going to be me. Besides, I haven't even thought it all through properly yet.'

'I'm calling him now.'

'Hey, butt out. I don't even know that putting my eggs on ice is the solution. If anything it might just be getting his hopes up. And like you say, it's painful, and just because I go through with it, it doesn't mean I'm ever going to change my mind about having kids. Please understand Rebecca, I know you're his friend but this has got to be between Mark and me.'

She blinks at me, like those dazed cats who wake up to find someone shaking a Kitty-Kat box over their head. 'No,' she explains. 'Not *Mark*. I'm going to tell Vagina Man that I'm pregnant. I can't believe I ever let you talk me into concealing my pregnancy from him.'

'*Moi*?'

'*Toi*! What were you thinking? Convincing me to tell the poor man that he's going to be a father on his own stag night. God Anna, that's the most hare-brained scheme I've ever heard.'

I open my mouth for a minute to defend myself but think better of it. Actually, I'm relieved to see she's coming to her senses about telling Rob. I definitely don't want to talk her out of it again.

'What kind of crazy idea is it, not telling the man of your dreams that you're going to have his baby?'

I agree that it is one hell of a crazy idea. Half of me is relieved that she is finally seeing sense, the other half fears for her. Only a very, very small part of me feels that I am being blamed unfairly.

She fondles her cell-phone. 'Should I phone him, or tell him to his face do you think?'

'To his face, definitely,' I counsel. 'Only finish your lunch first,' I urge, placing my hand over her phone. Besides thinking that telling him over the phone is a v. bad idea, I don't want to deal with the fall-out. 'Remember, you're eating for two now,' I remind her, guiding the phone back towards her bag and directing her fork, still laden with food, towards her mouth.

She seems to be complying as she takes the food into her mouth and begins to chew.

'Take him out to dinner tonight,' I suggest – like when I am way, way away from the fall-out. 'Somewhere really nice, and tell him about the baby over coffee.

'PS: Get him totally smashed first, though. Legless if at all poss. Then, just as he's enjoying his cappuccino, give him the happy tidings.'

She makes a sort of yelping sound and looks at me like I just suggested a murder-suicide pact for dessert. Then the food she was chewing goes everywhere. 'He doesn't drink coffee and nor do I now that I'm pregnant! God Anna, don't you know what coffee does to the foetus?'

'Um . . . perks it up?' I suggest gamely.

'You're insane Anna. I should never have listened to you in the first place. What do you know about marriage and kids anyway? I'm going to call him now.'

Before I can stop her the cell-phone is out of the bag and the numbers are being punched in. I watch her face go whiter and whiter as she drops her bombshell over the airwaves. Her eyes fill with tears and I feel helpless. Vagina Man takes it badly and hangs up.

'Maybe he just went into cell hell?' I offer feebly in the ensuing silence, but it doesn't stand up and Rebecca starts to lose it.

Really lose it.

In front of the whole Upper West Side restaurant; this charming bistro on Columbus in which, according to Rebecca, Vagina Man and she dine regularly. Maybe she figures after all the tipping she's done she is owed a scene. But a quick look around suggests that the management don't share her view.

And we aren't talking a few little sobs and a sniffle here. Oh no. We are talking a breakdown of catastrophic proportions, and the dozen or so shocked waiters who have come to view her as a friendly face and a reliable tip take her collapse really, really, badly. Looking at the expressions on their faces, I note that none of them are philosophical.

Suddenly the maître d' appears from nowhere and verbalises his irritation in a typically frank New York way. Not that it would be something I'd want in *my* restaurant, but I'm not quite certain what to do. I say a few soothing things along the lines of every cloud having a silver lining.

PS: I don't have time to be imaginative.

Rebecca, meanwhile, is simultaneously screaming, throwing her limbs around, smashing her head on the table and throwing plates at other diners. A normal display of Manhattan Stress Syndrome some might say, but apparently v. daring for the Upper West Side.

PS: So much for its reputation as a laid-back liberal area.

This isn't the East Village, their shocked faces seem to say, and absolutely no one even listens to my excuse that she is rehearsing a performance art piece. Not for a minute.

They threaten to call NYPD blue, actually.

A cell of waiters gather around us to shield the other diners from the unpleasantness of what started as garbled sobbing and recriminations (aimed mostly at me from what I could tell), progresses to coherent cries of 'Vagina Man! Vagina Man! Oh my God, Vagina Man!'

The maître d' asks me if I could be responsible for escorting my distressed friend home. He also mentions my paying the bill. But both tasks are easier said than done. For starters, Rebecca is distraught, *non compos mentis*, and over five foot ten if she's an inch. Secondly because of the way she is holding me, i.e. around the neck, I couldn't get to my purse even if I wanted to.

It is really lucky, as it happens, that Mark turns up when he does, and what with everything happening at once I don't bother inquiring as to how he came to be here on the other side of town from where he works and why he doesn't seem surprised to see us. I am too busy helping him get Rebecca into a cab where we have to sit on top of her so she can't do herself or anyone else an injury.

Back at her apartment, I make chamomile tea which hits her about as hard as a feather, so I dig up some vodka from the drinks cabinet and pour it down her neck with a funnel.

When she calms down, I start to explain to Mark what has happened, but as it turns out Vagina Man has already phoned him. Jubilant.

Incredibly, without even meaning to, I'd got it right – cell hell had struck again. Sometimes you can just get lucky with these mad excuses, I guess.

Rob walks in laden down with flowers just as Rebecca starts singing, 'You Make Me Feel Like A Natural Woman'.

PS: I may have been a bit heavy handed with the vodka so I really, really hope the baby's brain isn't in the process of forming.

CHAPTER TWENTY-NINE

Visiting someone's past is a bit like visiting communist China. First of all you need to obtain the appropriate permissions. Once in possession of a visa your movements will be strictly curtailed. Your sightseeing will be limited to wandering around the designated highlights and attractions as directed by your guide. If you venture into a non-designated area or ask too many questions, you run the risk of being forcibly removed.

Oh, and don't forget cultural activities and romantic history are protected areas and not open to outside criticism.

Extract from the 'New York Girl' column of Anna Denier

Mark

Anna is in jubilant mood and I hate to break her bubble.

'You know what, I've been thinking,' she begins. 'Maybe I've been too mad about this fear of motherhood thing—'

'Anna, don't. Listen to me, there's something I've been trying to tell you.'

As we wander into the evening, Anna is staring straight ahead as if she isn't listening to me at all, but I know she is. Even over the noise and activity of the street, I sense that you could hear a pin fall in her head.

'When Rebecca and I went away to the kibbutz,' I start off awkwardly. 'Dome Head and Rob went with us,' I add, so as she won't fixate on the Rebecca aspect and get thrown off the main point.

I'd planned every word I was going to say. I'd even gone over my speech with Bec. It was sad, that's what it was. But every day I'd allowed to go by without telling Anna the truth, made the confession seem bigger. Talking about it now, it sounded like it was all part of somebody else's life.

Like most guys I started my justifications up front. 'I mean, I should have told you this a long time ago but when do you start sharing secrets with the girl you're falling in love with?'

'When you start leaving a toothbrush,' Anna replies glibly.

I nod, it was what I'd decided myself. Leaving a toothbrush kind of signifies a commitment to keep coming back. Which is weird cause you can replace them for a buck.

I shove my hands into my pockets as the cold wind bites into them.

'God, where are all the taxis?' Anna asks, irritated.

But I don't let the interruption get in the way of my PR. 'Thing is right, in Israel you can sell your sperm. Twenty-five shekels was the going rate when we were there. Which is a nice supplement to the pathetic pocket-money wage of the kibbutz.'

'Gross.' She makes a revolted face that takes a metaphorical inch off my dick. 'You were one of those creeped-out guys who do it in paper cups?'

'Just the once.' It wasn't my finest hour, but I'm a lawyer – never admit when you're in the wrong. 'You make it sound sleazy,' I tell her, sounding all aggrieved. Put them on the defensive, especially when you're the one in the wrong. Don't let them smell the guilt.

'Jerking off in a paper cup in the Holy Land isn't sleazy?'

'Hey, it was for research. We were benefiting science.'

'Of course you were. Jerking off for science. How noble.'

'It wasn't anything to do with IV fertilisation,' I argue, spotting a cab and diving out into the street to hail it. The driver pulls over and we clamber in. 'It was to assist researchers in something or other. Something vital to the survival of the human race,' I assure her once I've told the taxi driver, 'Bleecker Street.'

'Did you look at pornographic magazines?' she inquires, as if she is doing her own research.

I don't want to go to that place right now, so I ignore the question. 'Dome Head was doing it every few days,' I throw in, once the cab is on its way. As if this somehow makes my own modest one-off donation more worthy.

'How impressive,' she mutters under her breath. Anna's never been very sympathetically disposed towards George.

'The thing was, they only accepted your um, semen, if there was sperm in it.'

'I don't get it.'

'Yes you do,' I tell her. I really don't want to split the atom, as Anna would say, over the difference between semen and sperm. Not in a New York cab after one of my best friends has trashed a restaurant. 'One's the carrier and one's the agent,' I explain.

She nods her head. 'You mean swimmers? The tadpole guys who rape the ovum.'

'I guess. Anyway, just let me finish.'

'Wait a minute. If they only accept your shot if there are swimmers in it, Dome Head must be extremely virile?'

'Yeah, whatever, but the thing is—'

'Doing it every few days, I mean.'

'Yes,' I agree. 'Virile. Normally they only let you go once every week because—'

'They say that bald guys are more virile than hirsute men so it just surprised me that it was true. Those things never are, are they?'

'What?' I'm getting irritated now.

'Truisms, they're very rarely true.'

'Can I just finish what I want to tell you?' I ask frustrated by how off-course we are getting.

'You want to tell me that you weren't, don't you? Weren't fertile, I mean. You want to tell me that they threw your little cup back in your face and didn't give you your twenty lousy shekels.'

'Twenty-five,' I correct. I feel the pores close up all over my body as she goes straight to the heart of what I'd been trying to tell her for months. 'You're sterile, aren't you, Mark?'

A siren flies past and I suddenly find myself totally engrossed in my hands. 'Yes, I'm sterile.'

'So when I had the pregnancy scare ... you thought ... ?'

'I didn't know what to think,' I mutter, aware of what I am admitting. I had believed Anna had been unfaithful and said nothing. I had concealed my doubts, knowing that I was making her feel guilty but unable to have it out because ... because why?

'You didn't know what to think?'

I am glad she is being agreeable. 'That's right. I was confused.'

'But you thought the worst?'

I gaze out the window of the cab at the grid-locked traffic. Motorists are leaning on their horns, the noise is deafening. My head is throbbing. Our own driver adds a blast of his horn to the cacophony.

'You thought I'd been screwing around? Didn't you?'

I don't have a convenient swipe-card answer. At least I do have an answer but I'm not particularly proud of it so I say nothing. That's what guys do, we'll always avoid an emotional challenge, dodge diffi-cult situations wherever we can. Non-confrontational, that's me. Is that so bad?

'So why did you stay with me? Why didn't you say anything?'

'I don't know.' I look at my hands as if I might have written crib notes on them earlier. 'I didn't want to lose you. I didn't want you to run off because it wasn't mine. I didn't know what to do.' I am telling the truth and it feels cleansing and liberating. Rebecca was right, it doesn't sound as bad when I say it. I am a nice guy. A noble guy. A guy who was prepared to shoulder the responsibility of another man's kid. This is okay.

'And because you felt guilty that you hadn't told me about your sterility in the first place, right?' she offers. 'And the reason you didn't tell me that you couldn't offer me kids is because that would have been the signal to talk about what you *could* offer me and you didn't want to go to that place – am I right?'

'Well, all girls want kids,' I remark lamely.

'You've been reading too many cereal boxes.'

I don't feel now would be the time to point out that she is the biggest cereal box reader of the two of us. I never eat cereal. Instead, I study her. She's staring out the window across the Hudson at the ships. She has the most amazing jaw line, it is set and firm and

I want to stroke it but I guess it isn't the time. I remember once when I was about four. I was in trouble for letting the rabbit out of its hutch. And my mother was threatening to tell my father when he got home. And looking sterner than I'd ever seen her look before. And I remember that I could smell her perfume and all I wanted to do was throw my arms around her and ask for a story and feel her hold me like she did when she put me to bed at night, but we weren't at that place.

I want to know what she is thinking and whether it is going to be alright. I touch her hand and she turns to me and says, 'You let me make a total fool of myself over this parenthood thing. Why couldn't you have told me?'

'I fucked up.'

'Fucked up? Fuck, Mark, you have no idea. The tears I've cried, the nights I couldn't sleep. You knew it was all because I thought *you* wanted kids. Why didn't you just say something?'

'I . . . I meant to . . . I—'

'Asshole!'

And I look at her and I don't know what to say. I can't relate to what I've done at all, but why not? It's my life, my secret. It's all my fault and I know it. I just want to get through this confession and take my punishment like a man. And get on with the rest of my life – hopefully with Anna.

'I don't know,' I repeat, as if the phrase is a key that I'm trying to turn in a stubborn lock. As if it's merely a matter of applying the right pressure to the vowel. 'I put it off for so long, the lie just grew and grew. It all got totally out of control. I didn't know you *never* wanted children. Not first up. All girls want kids, right? It's an instinct. So I kept it to myself, put off telling you in case telling you put you off me.'

She puts her hand on my leg and I wrap my hand around hers. It is like holding a detonator box – but at least it is my hand on the lever. I lift her hand to my heart and squeeze.

'Let's make up when we get back home,' she says, and I almost but not quite can't believe my ears.

'Is it really going to be okay?' I ask.

'Depends what you mean by okay. You know what Sienna says—'

'Truth is destiny?' I parrot, and we snog.

There was never any question that we'd end up in bed, we were tearing one another's clothes off before we got out of the taxi – it really was going to be alright.

The next day, after a leisurely breakfast reading the papers and one another's bodies, we got rugged up and walked through the park with our hands in one another's pockets.

I bought one of those disposable cameras from a kiosk and we took a roll of film, pretending to be geeky tourists in SoHo. We didn't mention my secret again. It was as if it had never happened. Only it had happened. I'd revealed my hand. I was the sort of guy who didn't own up, the sort of guy a girl like Anna couldn't trust to let her in, and it bugged me but what could I do?

Outside a gallery on Spring Street, we asked a group of Japanese tourists to take our photograph. Anna told me that at least now I was a shit she could be sure that my image would come out.

'I love you,' I whispered in her ear as we hugged.

But she didn't say the words back. She just said, 'You smell so good,' and snogged me. Which was a pretty okay substitute, I guess.

CHAPTER THIRTY

The stag night is the symbolic farewell to all the things that men feel life ought to have been, but never really was. A celebration of guyness, where they gorge on cigars and booze and testosterone. If you're a lucky stag, girls dressed up as bunnies will dive out of cakes for you and call you 'big-boy'.

The hen night is the night where girls kill the rumour that they are made of finer stuff than guys.

Extract from the 'New York Girl' column of Anna Denier

Anna

Oh shit.

I am stuck in my serialised dream again, only this time I am awake. Far too awake. Not so much as a blindfold, a pair of earplugs or a Valium to soften my fate. This is reality now and as anyone who lived through the eighties knows, Reality Hurts. Or is that Bytes? I am not really old enough to be turned into the eighties, I guess.

Why do people get married? Fear, loneliness, the dress, the photo opportunity, the presents, the party. I'm so *not* going to get married, I say, knowing that no one cares.

Sienna says that marriage is compromise, but then so's a rental agreement. So's travelling on the subway, and going to laundromats. So's paying rent. Despite all the advances of the last millennium, most people are still doing stuff they'd rather not be doing.

I close my eyes and take another sip of peppermint tea. I look over at Rebecca who is looking at her watch. Earlier on in the evening she toyed with the concept of learning to knit, but I threw a glass of iced water in her face which brought her round pretty sharpish. This is her hen night after all.

We are sitting alone in the green room, one of the three rooms hired for Rebecca and Vagina Man's stag-hen-combo. Gender-catered revelry rages on either side of us with no hint of flagging in the near future.

The planned green room entertainment – a cabaret act specialising in hits of the twenties – cancelled at the last minute. We've tried to watch television but with the party noise coming from the rooms either side, we are too distracted. Not that there is anything on. How sad are we?

Desperately sad, that's how sad.

Every time the laughter on either side of our room gets louder, I start to think that about the two-way mirror aspect of my dream. Even if there is a two-way mirror in the other two rooms, I doubt anyone would bother to peek at *us*.

Out of conscience, friendship and a host of other outdated loyalties, and the fact that I hate most of Rebecca's friends, I decide to stay here with her because the hen room is too smoky and noisy. She is also worried that the goings on might upset the foetus.

'Given that the foetus is stuck in the darkness of

your uterus, floating round a bucket of water with nothing to do other than suck its thumb,' I tell her, 'it would probably be glad of a few Chippendales.'

But Rebecca won't buy it. She muses out loud about whether I think Rob is satisfied with the entertainment she has provided for the stags. I look at her like she's mad. For the first time in my life I grasp what Freud meant by penis envy.

Given the outrageous amount of noise – cat calls, yahooing and cries of 'Get down' – I can only imagine that the *gatoys* are everything Vagina Man and his buddies ever dreamed of, and more.

In the suite on the other side, the girls-only festivities are reaching what I can only hope is the climax. If they get any more excited in there, they are going to come through the wall.

The hens' entertainment involves Playboy-esque bunny-girls walking around with cigar trays and Chippendale strippers walking around, in . . . well, let's face it, little more than a cock ring. Vagina Man has excelled himself. Every fibre of my being is trying to pull me in there, especially the Upper East Side girl, who is a little tramp if the truth be known.

Topsy attended my father's stag night. Obviously. Some sad leftover feminist of the period had written a book about it which never sold, entitled *The Real Story of the Stag*. I think a lot of naturalists bought it, thinking it was to be a nice tale of hunting in the forests of Oregon. Which of course it wasn't.

My father was cut up about it for years.

I suppose it must have come as a shock seeing Topsy armed to the teeth with the rent-a-rad-fem crowd she used to hang out with in the seventies. They turned up just as the strippers arrived, waving placards, declaring that men were animals.

Topsy et al set about bundling all the stripper bunnies into the backs of vans and spray painting all the stags. The night of my father's stag was one of my bedtime stories. I used to imagine my mother and her girlfriends raiding my father's party like a berserk brigade of animal rights activists attacking an animal testing lab. It sounded like a lot of fun to me at the time. Especially the part when all the bunnies were set free in the park.

It was a story told as a fairytale to me as a child around Easter. But that was years before I understood the Freudian-ness of it all.

THREE HOURS LATER

I don't know if I'm proud to admit it but my PC morality cells are still prevailing over my party-or-die cells. Rebecca has nodded off a few times but refuses to let me take her home.

'I'm not going to miss my own hen night, Anna! Don't be mad!' she shrieks every time she wakes up to find the porter guy and me trying to wheel her out to the lift in the luggage trolley.

Could I be any more bored? Let me see. I look around – no booze, no entertainment, stripped bare mini-bar, no light for my cigarette (can't smoke around pregnant girls anyway, the legal suits are enormous).

Could I be any more bored? Mmmm, let me see . . . No.

Listless and bored are to most girls on a par with living amongst Taliban militia. The concept of the green room was that men and women can both move freely without fear of being accosted by *gatoys* or men in cock rings. A room where couples could meet for a smooch and an eye-roll about the goings on in their respective gender rooms. Obviously we got that wrong. Very wrong.

There has been virtually nil traffic between the green room and the gender designated rooms. We assumed that based on extant gender friendships, the guys and girls would want to meet up for a gossip and a cuddle, but so far that hasn't happened.

Admittedly it is only two am, and the night is still technically young, but as yet not one guy has bothered to venture out from their room, and the only girl who wandered in was a Playboy bunny girl trying to sneak into the stag room.

We had a competition earlier about who could not look at their watches the longest. I won. Then we had a few rounds of who could not hold a glass up against the adjoining walls. I lost. We'd demolished the canapés in the first hour and now we were into the mini-bar.

'So anyway, it's great that Vagina Man took your pregnancy so well,' I say, trying to jolly things along. 'Mark said he's really stoked about it. Can't wait to throw the little thing in the air, symbolically freeing him to go out into the world and prosper.'

Bec's resting her chin in her hands, staring at the wall that adjoins the stag party. 'I didn't think they'd enjoy the *gatoys* that much,' she moans. 'I can't imagine what they're doing in there.'

'We could always gatecrash?' I suggest longingly, but she kills my hope with a look that could sterilise.

'Well it's better than strippers, that would have been just plain demeaning,' I offer.

'At least I'd know what the strippers were doing,' she points out. 'And let's not forget that he arranged strippers for my room. Do you think he was trying to demean me?'

'Um,' I prevaricate. 'Um, well I'm not sure about demean – that's a big ball park.'

I'm so glad when Mark saunters in that I dive into his arms before noticing his expression.

PS: Black with fury.

'Are you really going to freeze your eggs?' he asks me, noticeably unenthusiastic about my bear hug. He is looking like he's about to burst out of his clothes, turn into an action hero and start fighting evil. Only I'm not sure who the enemy is.

'How could you Anna?'

Okay, so I know who the enemy is. It's me. Little old bored and frustrated me. 'I thought you'd be pleased,' I mutter, eyes downcast.

PS: I'm hoping he'll think I'm too cute to be annoyed with.

'You bitch.'

But he's not.

'Why Anna? Why?'

'Well, I thought someone should stay with her on her hen night. I mean—'

'Why are you putting your eggs on ice?'

'Ah that. Well, see, Topsy—'

'You *know* I'm sterile.'

I cringe. 'Um.'

'Fuck Anna!'

'See, the thing is—'

'Who are you putting your eggs on ice for?'

'Well, the thing is . . . and then of course there is

. . . And the open option situation was a consideration and the . . .'

His face clouds over with a new look I don't recognise. And then I think I do – could it be contempt? I can't remember ever seeing his upper lip raised at the corner before. I try as hard as I can to pull my head down inside my body like those turtles do in cartoons. I'm not scared of his anger so much as his detachment. Detachment is the most lethal weapon in a lover's arsenal.

I cast him my most adorable smile ever. Where is Rebecca to back me up? I turn but she's just sitting there, shaking her head and making you-are-so-in-trouble faces at me.

'You know I'm sterile, so what's all this about? Who are you freezing these eggs *for*?'

'Who told you I was thinking about freezing my eggs anyway?' I demand, hedging the main issue like nobody's business.

'Does it matter?'

'Of course it does! There's the principle of the issue.'

'Principles?'

'Loyalty even. So go on, who told you?'

'Rob!'

I stand there spluttering, hoping I've heard wrong. 'Vagina Man?' I swing round to face Rebecca. 'Why

did you tell Rob? You, you, you . . . big fat betrayer!'
I yell at her, but she looks like she's about to cry and I
know it's not really her fault, or Rob's fault. It's mine.
All my fault. I should have said something.

Now as I look at Mark standing there in all his
detached disappointment, his expression retracting
every caress, every declaration of love, every kiss
he's ever shared with me, I want to turn back the
clock and have this conversation in bed together, with
him on top and me underneath, and then with me on
top and him underneath. I want to tell him why I am
considering this option while kissing all the whitest
parts of his torso.

Now the whitest part of his anatomy is his face. The
year-long golden tan of his complexion is bleached
with disappointment. 'How could you?' he repeats.

'Well you see—'

'I told you everything, Anna. Everything.'

'I did warn you he might get annoyed, Anna,'
Rebecca pipes up at the very moment Mark storms
out of the room. I look at her for help but all she can
do is shake her head ruefully. I run after him, only to
see the lift doors shut in my face.

By the time I do get out onto the street, his taxi's
driving away, and as it happens that is the last taxi I
see that night. I walk home through the quiet streets.
The tears streaming down my face feel like ice in the

freezing winds. I am wearing a beaded black strappy dress with my vintage coat over the top and I've never been so cold in my life.

When I finally get back to my apartment, my body's shivering through with chill and my trademark cigarette's frozen onto the skin of my lip. I run warm water from the bathroom faucet onto it but no amount of careful peeling will shift it. Bloody, buggery bum. I am going to have to have it surgically removed.

Accepting defeat, I light a fire in the grate and then I light the cigarette and cough like mad as I try and curl up on the mat like a cat. I can't stop my teeth chattering. Fuck my eggs, it's me who's on the rocks. As the flames lick menacing shadows around the room, I punch Topsy's number into the phone.

'Eggnog?' she asks sleepily.

'Oh Mom, everything's gone so awfully wrong.'

'Darling, what's happened?'

But just then I hear a key turn in the lock.

'Just a second,' I say, pushing the tears back into my eyes. Mark walks in, takes the phone from my hand and speaks into the receiver. 'It's okay Topsy, I've got it all under control, we'll call you back in the morning,' he tells her.

'I didn't mean to make you feel bad. I *do* see you in my future, you know. More than I see my own eggs actually,' I assure him, the cigarette making me sound like I have a fat lip. 'Topsy talked me into it as a means of reconciling me to you, and then after you told me—'

'Shhh,' he soothes, peeling off the cigarette and putting it out. Then, planting small warm kisses all over my frozen face, he tells me he loves me.

'I love you too,' I whisper, so quietly I doubt he hears me. I feel his heart pounding against my breasts. 'I love you too,' I repeat more bravely. And in the silence that follows, I feel like I've just dived off a cliff without a safety harness. It feels exhilarating and liberating and terrifying all at once. I've actually said the words. I've actually said the words and not vaporised into a pile of scatter cushions and home improvements.

'I love you too,' he whispers, and even though he's said it to me at least a thousand times before, it feels like I am hearing the words for the first time. Really hearing them. Then I hear Sienna's temple bells ringing in her apartment as he picks me up and carries me to the bedroom, and I think about Charles and her down there feeling this same stuff, and I don't feel nearly as annoyed about their relationship as I did.

CHAPTER THIRTY-ONE

I'm not a fool. I know the headline 'Topsy Denier's Daughter Takes Her Mother's Advice and Decides to Have Her Eggs on Ice' will appear in the paper one morning. A short time later the e-mail will flash across my screen.

Dear Anna,
How could you? How could you keep a story like that from me?
The Jerk.

Dear Jerk,
It was easy.
Anna Denier.

Anna

It's almost seven months later when I finally do the deed.

The decision whether or not to freeze my eggs took a long time to make, which is ironic given that I only considered it as an option to keep my options open. Go figure.

Mark wasn't a great supporter of the idea it has to be said. He was a shit about it for a while really, which both surprised and thrilled me because it proved that he was real after all. He was capable of feelings and emotions that weren't always of the godly kind.

Topsy is holding my hand, but not in the motherly way you'd imagine. She's actually looking at my nails and tutting. (Topsy's of course, are always perfect.) 'Eggnog,' she scolds. 'How do you let your nails get into this state? Don't they have manicurists near you?'

The truth is I have hardly left my keyboard in months. I have finished the first draft of my book, *Singled Out*, and even though I have gone through my advance with the speed of a breakfast espresso, I'm feeling pretty high about it. It has frequently been said that writing a book is like giving birth, so in that sense it was a dry run for me.

This procedure is my congratulations present.

'This is a sort of an anti-decision based on anti-commitment,' I explained to my readers in my last column. Did I mention that I threw my column in? Well, The Jerk threw me in, really. I just wasn't single enough anymore.

There is a doctor at the end of the bed – a woman, mercifully. Her name is Dr Kern and she is rummaging around inside me. Every so often she winces and then smiles as if she is plucking eyebrow hairs.

If I want to I can watch the procedure on the monitor, but the very idea of having someone moving things around inside me is spooky.

I'm in those stirrup things that they stick birthing women in. There is no way I would want to push a baby out suspended in this contraption. It reminds me of a picture I saw of torture devices used in the inquisition. I punch Rebecca's number out on my cell-phone. I must warn her about the stirrups. There is no way I'm going to have my friend give birth like this. No way.

The line's engaged so I keep punching in the numbers. While I'm waiting for her to answer and feeling as uncomfortable as all hell, Mark is on his knees proposing marriage.

Oh, didn't I mention that?

I'm answering in the negative. 'I'm an ubermodern girl, unencumbered and free. I don't need any more bits of paper restraining me in my life,' I declare.

'So you're not going to accept this incredibly huge diamond ring?' he asks, producing a velvet box.

'In your dreams,' I squeal, spotting the sparkle and snatching it from him faster than you can say 'Topsy Denier's daughter'.

'Okay, so that's it.' Dr Kern says, beaming.

'That's it? That's it?'

She repeats that it is, indeed, a wrap.

In five minutes I have joined that great archive of women who can't make up their mind. Women, girls even, who have found the overwhelming ability to gestate life inside their own body too terrifying to deal with in the near future. Girls who feel the pull of biology – but not enough to go with the tide. Surf girls.

'I hope they'll be alright,' I say to Topsy as she walks back in, having disappeared during Mark's proposal to get – what else – champagne. 'I hope they won't feel lonely. Or unloved. Or cold.'

I'm sure Topsy is about to say something really Topsyish but Rebecca finally answers her cell-phone.

'Okay,' I say urgently. 'Listen up Rebecca, this is really, really important. Whatever you do, I don't want you giving birth in the stirrup chamber, okay? You have to promise me that. They are, like, so demeaning and, well, uberbad news actually.' I have quite a bit more to say on the issue but she cuts me short.

'I'm in labour, Anna.'

'What?'

'Four minutes apart already,' she pants.

'Four minutes?' I shriek, knowing how short a gap four minutes is. Hell, you can have your eggs taken out in four minutes!

She screams down the phone in pain. 'Closer to three, really.'

'Where are you?'

'Rob's meeting me at the hospital, he's there now. I'm on the corner of Lexington and twenty-third in a taxi.'

'What are you doing there?'

'I went to have my nails done.'

Later, as we pass Alice Epstein around our group like a Christmas present, Rebecca looks like she's been spat out from one of those sausage-making machines. Rob looks like he could go a round with the world heavyweight champion. And now that I study him, he does look like the kind of guy to throw a baby in the air.

'She is sweet isn't she?' I concede, marvelling at her miniature hands and feet while Mark squeezes me and breathes kisses into my ear.

'She's got my nose,' Rob boasts, grinning inanely.

'But she's got my nails,' Rebecca points out, holding up a perfectly manicured hand for us to admire. On the battleground that is her body they stand out like jewels in an unmade bed, and Rob does something I never really thought he had in him and kisses her hand regally.

Topsy removes the cork from the Bollinger with a professional flourish. 'It's got to sigh like a virgin,' she says matter-of-factly and starts handing out glasses.

Rebecca reaches out to take Alice from Mark, and Rob sits down beside her, kissing both his wife and daughter on the head. I watch Mark looking on and I see what he sees, the perfect family unit, the ultimate consummation of love. I kiss him on the cheek as Topsy fills our glasses.

'It's incredible isn't it?' Mark whispers in my ear.

I nod, but actually I still don't get it. I can see how happy they all are, I can see the fulfilment in Rebecca and Rob's eyes, but I still don't get it.

Despite the polls I've read and all the pregnancy power banter in the media, I suspect there is probably no mother in me dying to get out. I suspect I'll always be the sort of girl who gets a kick sniffing the perfume seals in magazines, a girl who wears her cigarettes rather than smokes them, a girl propped up by little more than a Wonderbra and the hope that this season thighs will be in. And let's face it, these aren't the qualities kids are looking for in a mother.

But progress has been made. I have managed to say the words 'I love you', and if a guy taking a piss in the men's room were to ask me now, 'Where are you going?', I'd be able to give him a virtually clear indication.

TYNE O'CONNELL

What's a Girl to Do?

What's a successfully single girl to do when a trip to LA with her new lover lands her the lead role as the 'other' woman in another woman's relationship?

Evie's been single for like forever, and now she's finding that Coupledom is not nearly so simple as all those couples at parties make it look.

Ensconced in the celeb-packed Château Marmont hotel, where Greta Garbo lived and John Belushi died, Evie falls head over heels in love with the culture that coined the phrase 'shop till you drop'.

But she's hardly familiarised herself with the mini-bar before she has some tough decisions to make about how committed she's prepared to be – or for that matter, how single she wants to stay.

'Brings to mind Kathy Lette and Jilly Cooper' *Mail on Sunday*

'Lightning-fast comic twists' *Elle*

'Hilarious comedy of errors' *Good Book Guide*

'Makes *This Life* look tame' *Independent on Sunday*

0 7472 6028 1

review

TYNE O'CONNELL

Latest Accessory

Every modern woman knows the importance of getting her accessories right. This year, like most of the gorgeous young things in London with an overdraft and a Harvey Nichols chargecard, Evelyn is investing in a Prada handbag, saving up for a jacket by Alexander McQueen and thinking about a pierced navel. Somehow, though – without even needing to queue – she ends up with a stalker!

Evelyn, the lawyer with attitude and a penchant for Mr Wrongs, has moved into a loft in Clerkenwell and her anxiety levels are way up. She's got problems with debt, problems with builders, problems with her girlfriends, her love life and the usual problems at work. Add a stalker to the equation and you've got disaster. Or have you? Evelyn's about to find out that sometimes the solution is so much worse than the problem . . .

'Brings to mind Kathy Lette and Jilly Cooper'
Mail on Sunday

0 7472 5614 4

review

BEN RICHARDS

The Silver River

Nick Jordan is a young journalist who yearns for the big story.

Orlando Menoni is a cleaner from Uruguay who thinks back to the disappeared, and tries to come to terms with terrible loss.

This story of two very different men provides a moving and wholly original vision of the city in which the silver river takes on many meanings . . .

'Ben Richards's third book is all about the people who care, the people who don't yet, and the people who never will . . . Richards writes luminously about the grime and the glitter of London' *Independent*

'As suggestive and lyrical as it is pacy and slick' *Esquire*

'Refreshingly, Richards weaves his knowing sketches of London into a romantic South American tale of past revolution and lost love' *The Face*

'An intelligent, fast-paced read' *Mail on Sunday*

0 7472 5966 6

review

ISLA DEWAR

It Could Happen To You

Rowan has always cherished an ambition to travel. She didn't just leave the small Scottish town where she grew up; she fled from it as fast as she could. Now she's become expert at metropolitan living; she could walk by a million faces and not notice any of them. And her dream is almost within her grasp.

When Rowan does start packing her bags, she has to find room for one very unexpected item. And she's headed not for exotic distant shores but back to Scotland. There, she feels at first like nothing more than a source of good gossip. But as she discovers that no one is quite who she thought they were, Rowan begins to see that home could be where she'll find what she was looking for after all . . .

'Enchanting' *Options*

'Few writers are so good at making the reader empathise . . . Rowan is a delight' *Scotland on Sunday*

0 7472 5551 2

review